D0858817

PARANOIA

PARANOIA

A Novel

J. E. Braun

Tara,
I signed this since it's
now going to be a collector's edition!
:)

iUniverse, Inc.

New York Lincoln Shanghai

Paranoia

Copyright © 2008 by John Braun

All rights reserved. No part of this book may be used or reproduced by any
means, graphic, electronic, or mechanical, including photocopying,
recording, taping or by any information storage retrieval system without
the written permission of the publisher except in the case of brief
quotations embodied in critical articles and reviews.

iUniverse books may be ordered through booksellers or by contacting:

iUniverse
2021 Pine Lake Road, Suite 100
Lincoln, NE 68512
www.iuniverse.com
1-800-Authors (1-800-288-4677)

Because of the dynamic nature of the Internet, any Web addresses
or links contained in this book may have changed
since publication and may no longer be valid.

Certain characters in this work are historical figures, and certain events portrayed did
take place. However, this is a work of fiction. All of the other characters, names, and
events as well as all places, incidents, organizations, and dialogue in this novel are
either the products of the author's imagination or are used fictitiously.

ISBN: 978-0-595-47852-1

Printed in the United States of America

For my beautiful wife, Sharon,
and my two amazing children, Isabella and Caden.

Chapter One

My hands begin to shake a little and I realize that it's been a few days since that's happened, which is probably the longest stretch in years. I lay them, palm down, on the wooden railing and watch as they gently, but uncontrollably, jerk. Though my eyes are still a little weary, I try to focus on the scar on the back of my twitching hand. The redness has definitely diminished and the swelling has been gone for ages, but there's no doubt the mark will be visible for the rest of my life.

After a few moments, the shaking begins to make my stomach feel like it does when I try to read in the car, so I'm forced to look away and close my eyes until the nausea passes. When I open them again, the trembling has stopped.

The railing beneath my hands is chipped and the paint is faded. The whole wrap-around porch is, for that matter. I promise myself I'll fix it up as a favor to Aunt Beverly. After all, it's because of her generosity that I've been able to make it to a point where trembling hands is the worst of my problems.

When it first started, it only happened in the city or on public transportation—anywhere that drew a crowd of people. It used to be that I could experience the diligence and watchfulness that the government was calling for and still believe that it was just that, no matter how much it interfered with my ability to live my life "normally". It wasn't until it began to happen *everywhere* that I recognized it for what it was: simple fear and paranoia.

And by that time it was too late. They had won. At least with me, they had won.

The world today is not the same as the one in which I grew up and I'm not talking about the technology, though of course that has changed. I'm talking about the state of the world. Relationships between nations seem to be strained to their breaking points. At least when I was a kid, you knew who the enemy was: they were Russian, they had nukes, and they were located in the U.S.S.R. They had a country that we could theoretically attack and take over. That sort of thing would cripple an enemy. Sure, there were the nukes to worry about and, most likely, that's the reason nothing ever happened. My childhood was at the tail-end of the cold war. I saw the Soviet Union fall and the Berlin Wall torn to the ground. On television, I witnessed the massacre in Tiananmen Square. It was scary, without a doubt, but you knew your enemy. He was tangible. He could be stopped.

It's different now, though. The enemy does not belong to a country and no country belongs to the enemy. They are hidden, creative, and determined. I think that on a much greater scale, we feel like the British must have felt when the colonists began hiding behind trees and making sneak attacks. It's a whole new way of warfare that we just were not prepared for.

And we paid dearly. Thousands dead at the World Trade Center in New York City and at the Pentagon in Washington, D.C., not to mention Flight 93 outside of Pittsburgh on September 11, 2001. We didn't know what hit us. It was enough to make us all terrified.

I was at work that morning, bored, probably playing solitaire. My job had become an unchallenging routine, but that morning became anything but routine when a low droning noise in the distance gradually grew into a deafening roar. Whether you expect it or not, there is no mistaking the sound of a jet engine. The entire populace of the office moved so rapidly to the window it's a wonder the tower didn't tip over then and there. The shrieking began moments later. A couple of people fainted.

I was about halfway to the window when the building shook with a thunderous explosion that knocked every last person to the floor. On my way down, my head struck the corner of my desk and for a few moments consciousness eluded me. Struggling to focus, I fought through the throbbing pain in my head and pulled myself up into my chair. I placed my hand on the back of my head and luckily it came away with no blood.

All around me, lights were flickering and sparks were raining down in areas where fixtures had been dislodged. People around the office appeared to be screaming, but no sounds were registering in my ears. Within moments, first aid kits and fire extinguishers were being torn from the walls. The exit doors were jammed with people fighting to escape. Alarms must have been blaring because I could see the strobes flashing.

I will never be sure who it was, but in the chaos somebody grabbed my arm and dragged me to the exit. We shouldered our way into the flood of people in the staircase and descended God knows how many flights before my hearing started to return. I was just a block away when the plane hit the second tower. Before the debris began raining down, I tore my feet, heavy as concrete slabs themselves, from the sidewalk and ran like hell. I felt the rumble as the towers fell, but I never turned to look.

That was years ago, now. Today, watching the sun rise over the proverbial amber waves of grain in the Midwest, I feel only slightly better than I did then. Being out here has alleviated the fear a little bit, but every truck that goes by, in my mind, might be a nuclear bomb on its way to some major city. Depression is the problem *du jour*, but flashbacks still haunt me.

In the past few years, the question has arisen more than once, but I've never been able to answer exactly when it got so bad. Today is no different as I struggle to remember. I stare blankly out across the farm-land, watching the corn sway in the breeze and my eyes lose focus while my mind reels through the archives, playing moment after moment of my life. It's funny, but I can't remember ever not being scared. I know I wasn't always this way, but I can't remember that time of my life.

The breeze picks up a little and my hair flutters about my face. I don't try to keep it down or fix it. These days it's always too long and unkempt. My scruff grows well beyond a five o'clock shadow before I even think of taking a razor to it. In the past three months I think I've had two full-blown beards. Right now, the stubble is thick and dark, somewhere between the five o'clock shadow and the beard.

I'm wearing a flannel shirt, which seems to be my uniform of choice. I have nobody to impress and if I do happen to manage an honest day's work, the flannel holds up well. Out here, the only work you can get is manual labor. I don't work often, but when I do, I sweat. I don't enjoy busting my ass like that, but it sure keeps the mind in check. The jeans and work boots complete the ensemble and for a minute I have an image of myself walking up a runway like a fashion model, but the humorous image shatters when the word runway reminds me of an airport and an airport reminds me of that day.

I shudder as a humorous image in my mind's eye deteriorates into a hellish nightmare. That train of thought, that mental chain of events, is all too common. It doesn't take much to get me thinking about that day. Little, ordinary things make me remember 9/11 on a regular basis. Actually, remember isn't the right word, exactly. Immerse is the right word. I can be on the verge of a happy moment when suddenly I immerse myself in the past—I am temporarily removed from this more forgiving reality and thrust into the harsh world of Jim's life—my life—just after the towers fell. I am forced to re-suffer the experience in surround-sound and high-definition. Now is real and then is real and repeatedly the twain shall meet.

The porch boards creak behind me, which means Aunt Beverly is awake. She is the only one that is ever awake with me at this hour. For a farmer, my uncle sleeps awfully late, but that's the only trait he doesn't share with your stereotypical farmer. Stern, hard-working, and the last in a long line of farmers, Uncle Clint cannot accept weakness in a man, physical or otherwise. Family values are of the utmost importance to him. My life irritates him.

Aunt Beverly will talk to me for a few minutes and make sure that I am okay, and then she'll be off to feed the chickens and the pigs and milk the cow. Long after the rooster has gone down for a morning nap, Uncle Clint will get up and begin plowing the small field that has yet to be sold off. He won't stop to make sure I'm okay. Fact of the matter is, he doesn't really seem to care because I'm not his blood. Aunt Beverly is my mother's sister. My mother was on the seventy-eighth floor of the north tower of the World Trade Center on September 11, 2001, forty stories above me. She never made it out.

I didn't worry about her during my escape because Mom didn't normally work on Tuesdays. It was one of her days to work from home, but, for some reason I will never know, she went into the office that morning. I look at Aunt Beverly with a tear welling in my eye and I don't have to say a word because she knows who I'm thinking about. This time of day it's always Mom. After dinner, it's usually Rebecca and Andrew. I didn't lose them on September 11th, but I guess I lost them *because* of September 11th.

I turn away again and look back across the field. Aunt Beverly comes up behind me and wraps her arms around me. She gives a squeeze which says that she is genuinely happy to have me here, then she shivers.

"You'll catch your death out here," she says, and her voice, though just a whisper, seems to carry on forever across the farm.

"Do people really say that?" I ask with a chuckle. She laughs, too, and I realize just how infrequent that sound is. She misses her sister.

"Well I don't know about other people, but I do," she replies, finally letting me free of her embrace. And with that, the only family I have left turns and walks away. I listen to the sound of her footsteps on the porch boards fade away as she turns the corner down at the other end of the house.

But as her steps fade, others take their place. As the seconds pass, I'm hearing more and more footsteps. Lots of footsteps. High heels across a linoleum floor. Dress shoes. Even the soft slap of a pair of running sneakers doing their intended job.

I'm no longer on the farm. I'm in Penn Station in Manhattan. It's Friday, September 28, 2001.

I'm watching the world walk by as I bite into a slice of pizza that I bought from one of a half-dozen nearly identical subterranean restaurants. Next to the plate is a small mountain of napkins soaked in pizza grease. I can't bite into a delicious wedge of bread, sauce, and cheese without dabbing it repeatedly with napkins. I used to be able to eat it right out of the oven, but ever since that first dab of the napkin it's become more of an obsession than anything else. By the time I'm done, there is probably more paper on the slice than there is garlic or crushed red pepper.

The counter faces the corridor where people wait to find out the track number on which their train is arriving. I scan the crowd. It's so soon after 9/11 that people are still jumpy. Suspicious eyes dart every which way while mothers drag their small children through the crowds by their tiny hands. Young as those children are, they're still terrified; the images of planes crashing into the World Trade Center have been forever etched into their brains by CNN and Fox News long before their minds could possibly understand what it all means. Watching those children with their mothers makes me think of my mother who is still missing. She wasn't supposed to be at the office that Tuesday, but I was. I made it out and she might not have, but I try to push that thought from my mind. She is okay, I assure myself. She is going to turn up.

Out in the concourse, Arabs and other Middle-Eastern people practically tip-toe their way through the throng of travelers. The number of personal attacks on these people has risen drastically over the past few weeks and they seem acutely aware of each and every pair of eyes in the station crawling over their skin. I can't honestly say that *my* eyes aren't among them.

After a while, I stop noticing the panicking mothers and the jittery students as my full attention focuses on the Afghanis or Iraqis or Arabs, as if I could tell any of them apart. In my mind, though, not only can I distinguish between the nationalities, I can also discern the terrorists from the innocents. Piece of cake.

I'm not nervous about it at this point. In fact, I can even be slightly amused by my thoughts. I know that not every foreigner is a terrorist, but scenarios run through my mind—scenarios that seem to consistently end with me rushing from the depths of Penn Station, emerging into daylight near the steps of Madison Square Garden with a cloud of dust and smoke rolling through the exit all around me. Maybe one or two other people make it out. Maybe not.

I glance down at the counter and notice my pizza is gone. Only the taste of garlic on my tongue keeps me from thinking that someone swiped it from me. I guess I was eating on autopilot. With the last clean napkin, I wipe the corners of my mouth, then fold all of my trash into the paper plate. Apparently, I'm not the only one convinced that the trash can is able to take just one more thing. The receptacle is overflowing, but I try to stuff my garbage into the flap anyway while attempting to not actually touch anything. Judging by the dozens of wads of chewing gum stuck to the back of the cover, it's been ages since anybody has washed this thing.

Exiting the pizza place, I'm almost run down by two teenage boys sprinting through the concourse, probably late for a train. I'm in one piece only because I heard their fast footsteps approaching and jumped back into the pizza place. In my mind, the footsteps belonged to some terrorist who was about to tackle me. The terrified look on my face might have been comical in another time and place, but those who notice completely understand. I watch the two boys disappear through a couple of chrome and glass doors, joking and laughing with each other in a way that nobody else in the train station seems to be able to do. I vow to look both ways before leaving a pizza place from now on.

When I'm ten yards from the restaurant, I realize I left my backpack under the counter. I make my way back and pick it up off of the grimy, brown tile floor, not once considering that perhaps somebody had seen me leave it there and thought *I* was a terrorist leaving a bomb behind. Why would they? I'm obviously no terrorist. I heave the bulky black canvas sack over my shoulder and weave my way through the rest of the pedestrians. The timetable shows that my train is on time and boarding, so I hurry to the platform.

The air down here (another level below the subterranean pizza parlor) is heavy with exhaust, but the ventilation is working overtime to keep us from getting headaches, nausea and all of the other good stuff that can come from inhaling too many fumes. I glance up at one of the ventilation grates and think: only a little reversal of the system with a biological agent added and we're all dead. Maybe it's smallpox, maybe the plague. I'm not even sure the plague can be transferred through the air, or smallpox for that matter, but I figure the terrorists know what they're doing.

I board the train, find a nice quiet seat next to a very American-looking man (read: not Muslim) and dive into my newspaper. There are still plenty of articles about the attacks and the hunt for Osama bin Laden to keep the fear fresh in my mind, as if I needed any help. I skim those articles and look forward to the comics and the sports section, but *Garfield* seems less funny these days and the *Family Circus* always sucked. The Mets aren't in the post-season just one year after their poor showing in the subway series so I try to focus on the NFL which is one week behind schedule since they cancelled all the games the week of the attacks. Poor taste, they figured. The country wasn't ready, they said. I say entertainment is exactly what we need, but who am I?

As the train begins to ease its way out of Penn Station, I let the distraction of the newspaper take hold. The terrorists have slipped my mind temporarily. The station is not going to be gassed. The train is not going to blow up. I will not be murdered in a hijacking. Yet, somehow I know I'll feel even more comfortable when I arrive for my afternoon shift at our temporary offices in Newark, New Jersey.

CHAPTER TWO

"Suppertime, Jim," calls the melodious voice of Aunt Beverly. With my eyes closed and only my ears to guide me, she could be my mother. With my eyes open, there is enough resemblance to be a constant reminder. I step away from the wooden railing and realize that the sun has moved directly overhead. Jesus, have I been standing here that long? Uncle Clint walks by, glances at me and shakes his oversized head. He opens the squeaky screen door and goes into the house, his silence saying so much more about his feelings for me than words ever could. I bear it, though, and he does not voice his opinion—all for Aunt Beverly's sake.

I start to head to the washroom, but realize that I have done nothing that would require washing, so I head right for the dining room. Some families never use their formal dining room unless it's a holiday or a special occasion. Here, it is the only place you eat. Never outside, never in front of the television, and Heaven-forbid you even suggest the need for a dinette set in the kitchen. The dining room will do just fine, thank you very much.

I pull a chair out and take a seat as far from Uncle Clint as the dining arrangements will allow. The simple cherry wood table is long, so distance is not a problem. A single runner adorned with flowers and fruit, hand sewn by Aunt Beverly, is the only decoration. Steaming chicken and dumplings are placed before me. Lunch used to consist of McDonald's fries and a soda if anything at all. With meals like this, you would think that I would be packing on the pounds. I'm not. "Wasting away" is the term I hear most often.

Uncle Clint says grace before we dig into the meal. He asks the Lord to bless these thy gifts and so on and so forth. I suffer through it. Even if I did believe, I don't think Uncle Clint actually includes *me* in the blessing. Well, unless it goes something like: "Bless us, O Lord, for these thy gifts, except the ones sitting in front of Jim. If you could make them poisonous to rid me of this burden, that would be just fine. Amen."

There is a brief silence and then the clinking of forks on china is all that can be heard. Conversation doesn't exactly flow around here, not even between Aunt Beverly and Uncle Clint. Well, not in front of me, at least. I listen to their forks make music while mine still rests on the cherry wood. The sound increases in volume and then in tempo. The crescendo of silverware quickly becomes a cacophony until, just as I'm about to cover my ears to block the noise out, it becomes bearable again. It's bearable because they are not the forks of Aunt Beverly and the beloved Uncle Clint. I am back in my Manhattan apartment and they are the forks of Rebecca and Andrew. Tears well up in my eyes during that brief moment between when I know that the image isn't real and when I fully, if not temporarily, accept it as reality.

My fork rests on the linen tablecloth, untouched. I'm watching my wife and my son shovel food into their mouths like it's the first meal they've eaten in days, maybe weeks. I get an extremely fulfilling feeling from all this. It's been a while since I cooked a meal for them. Rebecca is home so much earlier than I am that it doesn't make sense for me to cook. Her food is wonderful, but this is a treat for them: Andrew because it's something different, Rebecca because she didn't have to cook.

Before I reach for my fork, I lean down and grab the newspapers that are stacked next to my chair: one *New York Times*, one *Daily News*, and one *Newark Star Ledger*. I place them on the table next to my plate and open the *Ledger*, snapping it rigid. Then the forks stop. Noticing the silence, I glance up over the top of the front page to see my family staring at me.

"What?" I ask.

"Jim," Rebecca says, pleadingly, "can't we get through one dinner without listening to you read us tragic news?"

"Sweetie, this is what's going on in the world. You can't look anywhere without seeing news about what happened a few weeks ago."

"Which is exactly why I'd like to just go one meal without it!" she hollers, obviously exasperated. Then she adds, "And stop being so damned condescending."

I shake my head. I can't believe what I'm hearing. How can they want to be so blind to what's going on around them?

"Listen, Becky, it's important ...,"

"If you won't do it because I asked," she interrupts, "do it because you're scaring the hell out of your son."

"Mom," Andrew begins, embarrassed, but Rebecca's glare silences him quickly. She's always been so good at that.

She focuses her attention back to me, then arches her eyebrow in a *Well, what are you going to do?* kind-of-way. I hesitate, but I know that understanding what is going on in the world transcends being scared. I intend for my son to be well-versed in current events. I want to know that he understands history so he can help prevent it from repeating itself.

"Andrew, you want to hear it, right?" I ask. Stupid, I know, but I ask anyway.

"Yeah, Dad," he says. If I would stop to think about him instead of me, I would realize how insincere that *Yeah, Dad* is, but I don't.

"Fine," Rebecca says, clearing her plate from the table.

She walks into the kitchen and drops the plate into the sink, then takes a deep breath and pushes her hair back out of her face. By this point I'm standing behind her and she knows it.

"Becky, this is impo ..."

"Andrew got in a fight today," she interrupts.

I look over my shoulder at my boy who is toying with the dinner he barely touched.

"Why?"

"Why? Why. Let's see," she says, turning to face me. "Apparently, Andrew was preaching about terrorism. About the government and how they're not going to protect us. People are still scared, Jim. Kids are scared. Some of the boys didn't want to hear any more, but Andrew was trying to make his Daddy proud."

"Don't put this on me," I snap.

"Then who? Who else is putting this stuff in his head?"

I don't try to argue her point. He did it because of me, but I just don't see it as a bad thing.

"The point is, those boys who are angry with him now will be dying at the hands of terrorists while our son is keeping himself safe."

She looks at me like she would look at a filthy, crazy homeless man who had tried to put his hands on our son, but then her shoulders slump, her glare softens and she turns back to the sink.

"Do what you want," she says without looking at me. "If you want to scar your son for life, go ahead, just don't blame me when he wakes up with nightmares every night."

"Nightmares? You don't know a thing about nightmares!" I cry. She freezes, knowing she chose the wrong words. I could go on, but it's not the direction in which this needs to go.

I walk up directly behind her and wrap my arms around her. The last remnants of apricot from her morning shower linger in her hair.

"You know what we have nightmares about? The unknown. Things we can't understand. Those are the things that make us the most anxious and frightened. We can't protect him from reality, Becky. But even though we can't protect him, we *can* prepare him—arm him—with knowledge."

She grabs my hands in hers and turns around to face me. Damn, do I love those eyes. Emerald. Well, they're definitely some shade of green, but emerald sounds so much better.

"What are you talking about?" she asks. Her voice comes out in a whisper even though I'm sure it wasn't intentional.

"What if he goes to school one day and hears some kid saying that the terrorists have decided to blow up all of the schools that day?"

I can feel her shudder at the thought. That's her weakness. She doesn't think of these things. They can happen, though.

"Would you rather he live in fear that day? Thinking we abandoned him to be slaughtered? No. I'd want him to be able to turn and tell them that it wasn't true—that intelligence indicates that there is no threat to schools or something like that."

"I don't want him to be scared," she says with a slight tremor in her voice.

"Me neither. So let's make sure he isn't."

The mental wounds of 9/11 are still bleeding, open sores. Maybe that's why she agrees, because normally I'm not very persuasive.

I kiss my wife and make my way back to the dining room where my son is sitting quietly. He looks up at me when I walk into the room with eyes that ask a million questions. If anyone is ready to learn, it is my son. I pull out the chair next to him and sit down. Opening the newspaper, I glance at Andrew to see if he is ready and he nods.

"EPA and OSHA declare the air near Ground Zero safe to breathe," I read. What a farce.

"I don't buy it," I say to Andrew as I scan the rest of the article. "Just the government trying to keep us all complacent." I drone on and on. Very little of it is news. Maybe a headline here or there. Most of it is commentary. Most of it is my extremely cynical opinion. By the look in his eyes I know that Andrew hears every word I say. What I don't realize is that, standing behind me, Rebecca does, too.

"Jim, have you had enough?"

On the verge of reminding Rebecca that this isn't for me, I hesitate. The voice, though familiar, isn't hers. I blink rapidly and look around. Aunt Beverly is standing next to me, holding my nearly-full plate. Uncle Clint is no longer at the table.

"Earth to Jim," she says.

"Sorry. Yeah, I've had enough. Thanks."

CHAPTER THREE

After lunch, I make my way to the barn to do some chores. There's a bit of guilt festering after wasting the entire morning, so the least I can do is try to be a little productive, but as I'm walking to the barn I run into Ray Peterson. Mr. Peterson is our nearest neighbor and runs a furniture restoration shop out of his barn a half-mile up the road. His face is wrinkled and ruddy, which makes him look like he's had a bit too much to drink even when he hasn't had a sip.

"Good Afternoon, Jim," he says, tipping his baseball cap.

"So I hear," I say.

He nods then looks around. "Seen Clint?" he asks, scanning the property.

"A few minutes ago. We had lunch. He doesn't know you're here?"

Mr. Peterson shakes his head then indicates for me to come with him. I follow him over to the barn, a bit wary of what he might have to say. We've already exchanged more words than we ever have in any one conversation.

"I was up in the city gettin' some paint and supplies when Jack Hadley tells me that some guy's been goin' around to the local businesses, showing your picture around, askin' about you."

"About me?" I ask as nausea begins to claw at the insides of my stomach. "You're sure?"

Mr. Peterson nods.

"Did he say who he was? What did Mr. Hadley tell him?"

"Well, told him he didn't know you, of course. The guy wouldn't give his name and didn't seem to know too much about you. Jack figured it would be some time before he figured out where you were, what with you not havin' the same last name as Bev. He left this."

He hands me a business card for a private detective.

My mind starts racing as every one of my muscles becomes tense. A private detective is looking for me and he's managed to track me to Colorado Springs. Images begin to flash in my skull: a shopping mall, a group of middle-aged men in a frenzy, and one particular face surrounded by greasy, jet-black hair. Stories, alibis and excuses begin to form, but I make myself believe I've done nothing wrong. *After all, the law wouldn't use a private detective*, I reason, in an attempt to calm my nerves. *Though, somebody seeking revenge might.*

"Any idea who he might be? It won't be long before somebody points him in the right direction."

Mr. Peterson studies me, obviously trying to read my expression. I shake my head in a lie that couldn't be more blatant, but he accepts it. He has been friends with Uncle Clint and Aunt Beverly for longer than I have been alive and protecting Aunt Beverly's blood is no different than protecting Aunt Beverly.

Uncle Clint comes around the corner and waves at Mr. Peterson. Mr. Peterson returns the wave then whispers, "I'll let you know if I hear anything. In the meantime, you may want to stay close to the farm."

I nod and thank him before he joins my uncle. I stare after him, but suddenly feel terribly alone as they turn the corner of the house. I look to the road, then out across the fields. Standing out here in the open makes me feel extremely exposed like I've got a sniper's cross-hairs trained on me. I try to sprint to the barn, kicking up dust and almost tripping over my own feet as they don't respond quickly enough to my brain's call for survival.

The barn is old and unpainted and the door creaks loudly when it's opened. I'm not sure how that sound hasn't driven the animals crazy. It grates on *my* nerves and I only hear it once every few days. Then again, I only come into the barn when I'm doing chores to help out Uncle Clint, which automatically puts me in a foul mood that no door is going to improve or worsen.

Scrunching up my nose, I look around and try to figure out what to do. I'll never get used to the foul stench in the barn, despite its becoming a part of my everyday life. The cow has been milked, the pigs have been fed, and I'm sure that whatever it is you do with chickens has been done. I did some work on the tractor yesterday and trying to do any touch-up work on the barn would be like spraying some air freshener at the local dump to make it smell pretty. I let out a deep sigh and run my hand back through my hair.

On the floor near the wall is a small milking stool. I set it upright and sit down. It's not the most comfortable seat in the world but it will do. Trying to block out thoughts of the detective, my mind starts to wander to the hay on the ground, the spider-webs in the corners, and the old rusty farm tools hanging on the walls. Studying the ordinary is a technique I use to help achieve a state of peace. Sometimes, like now, it works.

Until it comes. We live in the flight path of the airport, so I expect it to happen at least a couple of times a day. The distant hum grows gradually, until it swells into a whistling roar overhead. I race to the window and glance upward, staying to the side of the glass as if anyone thousands of feet in the air could see me watching them. I know paying attention to the sound of the airplane, or watching it pass by, is detrimental to all of the progress I've made so far, but I need to watch. I need to listen. I need to know that the plane is going to pass safely by.

Eventually, it does.

Sometime in the last thirty seconds, I broke into a nervous sweat. I can feel it on my brow and my shirt is sticking to my armpits. I wave my arms in large circles trying to dry out, but it just increases the discomfort. I also realize, from the dull ache in my jaw, that my teeth have been clenched since I first heard the plane overhead. I pry them apart and move my jaw in circles to loosen it up. Damn, sometimes I really hate myself.

Only sometimes? a voice in my head mutters with a distinct air of sarcasm.

"Shut up," I mumble, as I make my way back to the milking stool.

I stretch my legs back and tilt the stool until my shoulders rest against the rough planks of the barn wall. To my right, one of the planks has a series of knots lined up almost perfectly in a row. I reach out to touch one, but when my finger makes contact, it's with a glowing white circle with the number fifteen on it. I pull my hand back and look around. It's only a moment before I'm surrounded with my old co-workers in the company elevator.

"I hate this office," Jeff whispers to me.

"Huh?" I utter.

"The Manhattan one was so much nicer."

"I guess," I whisper back, wondering why it is we're whispering.

"What's the matter?" Jeff asks.

"Nothing, I guess," I lie, trying to ignore the urge to punch my fist into the emergency stop button. I also resist the urge to check to see if the emergency phone is operational.

"Dude," Jeff says, in his ever reassuring way, "it's been weeks. We're in Newark, New Jersey. The building is only 18 stories and of *no* importance. What the hell are you worried about?"

"I just wish I could be as confident as you."

The shifting and fidgeting in my peripheral vision tells me that our fellow passengers are beginning to become unsettled by our conversation, so I shut-up. Far be it from me to upset anybody.

The doors open on the twelfth floor and everybody exits except Jeff and me. I'm pretty sure some of those people work up on our floor, but I can't blame them for leaving early. The long elevator ride makes me jumpy, too. A moment later, the bell dings to announce our arrival on floor fifteen and we exit into the reception area of the office. Janet, the receptionist, offers her usual smile—the one that says, *I feel really bad for you guys, I do, but I can't wait until you're all out of my office. Does that make me a bad person?* The phone rings and she quickly grabs it. Too quickly. It's strange, but nobody knows how to act around us yet.

As we walk down the hallway, the co-workers we pass smile and nod at us without skipping a beat in their conversations. Our cubicle is in the far corner. Despite the company's best attempt to make everyone feel comfortable, our work environment leaves a lot to be desired. It's warm, overcrowded, and probably could have used a good cleaning even before we moved in, but of course nobody was prepared for what happened.

Jeff and I slide into our respective chairs in our shared cubicle. We have flat screen monitors that were given to us in an attempt to conserve space, yet every time Jeff and I shift in our seats, our chairs collide.

"So what is it you're actually afraid of?" Jeff asks. I know exactly what he is talking about, but I feign ignorance.

"Afraid?" I ask, innocently.

"Oh, please, Jim. You think I don't see how you're behaving?" His screen beeps to life and for a brief second he forgets about me while he types in his password. What I wouldn't give to freeze this moment so that the ensuing conversation would never have to happen.

"Look," I say, "it's a time of upheaval. Things just aren't normal. We can suffer another attack any day."

"Jim, look around you," Jeff says, waving his arms around the cubicle, as if the gray fabric walls were grand vistas replete with vast plains, wide rolling rivers, and snow-capped mountains. "Things aren't so bad. The Dow is back up over pre-attack levels, that guy from Pennsylvania is setting up that Homeland Security thing, the government is bailing out the airline industry, and we're probably days away from getting bin Laden. We're not going to see any more attacks."

I don't dare turn to look at him and risk exposing my true thoughts: that my cubicle partner, Jeff MacMillan, is a complete and utter idiot. How can somebody whose life would have been snuffed out on 9/11 if it hadn't been for subway delays be so delusional? It's not that I don't like him, but how do you go through life wearing such blinders?

"I'd like to believe that," I reply, pulling a can of compressed air from the drawer and blowing all the little food particles out from between the keys on the keyboard. "I would. But man, that's the exact kind of thinking that got the Trade Center knocked down in the first place. It's that 'It can't happen to me' attitude on a grand scale."

"Well, whatever. I don't know about you, but I intend to live my life and no scraggly-looking, bed-sheet wearing son-of-a-bitch is going to change that. If I let them, well, then they've won, y'know?"

"Yeah, I know."

It's been something like ten working days since Jeff and I moved into this office, and we've have had this conversation exactly ten times. It's almost a competition now, to see who can sway the other to their side first. So far, we've done nothing but solidify our own opinions.

I punch my login and password into the keyboard and wait for everything to load up. Jeff and I remain silent now, hearing, but not listening to the muffled phone conversations occurring throughout the office. With twice as many people in the office as we would normally have, there are still only half as many conversations. Sales are in a slump. I guess people think things like software are frivolous when there's so much violence in the world.

I glance to my right and watch Jeff begin editing lines of code. It's exactly what I should be doing, but instead I open an internet browser. *CNN.com. FoxNews.com. USAToday.com.* As usual, I notice they're all reporting the same canned news with just a slightly different political slant or an extra pie-chart, so I hit the newsgroups. Here's what I'm looking for. Bush knew about the attacks before they happened. The U.S. had Bin Laden cornered but let him go. There's something to be said for some of these kooks. They're not afraid to say the things that everyone else is afraid to say. True or not, they're not afraid.

I'm so engrossed in the articles that I actually jump out of my chair when my boss says my name. I hate when he sneaks up like that, especially when I'm not doing work.

"Yeah, Tom," I say, as casually as possible, trying to clear my screen without being conspicuous. He sees it, though, and it's not the first time.

Tom shakes his head and lets out a huff. "C'mon, Jim," he pleads. "It's been difficult to get everyone to focus and produce. When the sales team actually gets calls, our people have no passion. Our programmers zone out for minutes at a time. QA/QC has been letting more bugs through than ever."

I look at him without expression, waiting for him to finish his lecture. He's not a bad guy, really. I know I put him in this spot. I don't mean to, but sometimes I just can't focus.

"The point is, Jim, that at least they're trying. I can excuse poor performance when I know they're giving it their all. I can't when I know the employee isn't even making an attempt. Do you get what I'm saying?"

I nod. That's all I want to give right now. I reach over and click the mouse. The newsgroup disappears. I double-click and a window opens up, displaying lines of code. I raise my eyebrows to my boss and he nods before slinking away. Jeff, who was of no use during that entire exchange, is just tap-tap-tapping away at his keyboard and shaking his head. I ignore him because I don't need another lecture.

A moment later, the code disappears and the newsgroup is back. I just need to be more vigilant. I need to be more aware of when my boss is sneaking up on me.

"Jesus, man," Jeff says, "you're really asking for it aren't you?"

I shrug. "You'd do the same thing for something that you felt was important."

"Risk my job? Not if it was pointless. That's the thing, Jim. You can read all you want. You can study your conspiracy theories twenty-four hours a day. What good is it doing?"

"It's keeping me informed. Maybe even a step ahead of *them*."

"Maybe so, but regardless, if Tom catches you, he's going to throw you out on your fat ass."

I try to ignore him, but the problem is that he doesn't sound at all like himself. That voice: it isn't Jeff, it's Uncle Clint.

"I said, 'It would be nice if you'd get up off your fat ass.' There are things that need to be done around here," he says in his usual friendly manner.

I grunt a reply without looking at him. I know all too well what he looks like: rosy nose and droopy jowls; a pudgy face; gray hair over the ears, but completely bald on top; and uncontrollable ear hair. What Aunt Beverly ever saw in him, I have a hard time imagining. It certainly wasn't his good-hearted nature.

Uncle Clint continues to ramble on about something or other. I don't pay attention to the words, but he sure is making angry sounds. Without humoring him even the slightest bit, I rise from the stool and walk out of the barn. It's not like I'm risking getting him angry. He hates me for Christ's sake. That bridge is already burnt.

Chapter Four

Brooding in my room usually takes up a good hour or two each day. Aunt Beverly thinks I'm in here praying or doing something that a good Christian would do, but most of the time I'm staring at the floral pattern on the wall and other productive things such as that. The wallpaper pattern that has received much of my scrutiny is very subtle unlike the one on the sheets and pillow cases.

It's not a very masculine room, but then again it was never meant for me. It was never meant for anyone, really, since my aunt and uncle never had any children. I think any child would have been blessed to have Aunt Beverly as a mother, but equally cursed to have Uncle Clint as a father. Who knows, though? Maybe he would have been different with his own kids. Either way, it's better for whoever that child would have been. Being born into this world is not the prize it once was. I still worry about Andrew every day and wonder if I did him a disservice by having him in the first place.

The stream of light pouring through the window slowly extends across the hardwood floor of my room as the sun moves its way west. I missed a lot of beautiful sunsets over the mountains for the first few months that I lived here. I wanted to watch the glowing orb slide behind the peaks in a beautiful splash of oranges and reds, but I was always afraid that I would see a mushroom cloud form on the horizon. Denver, Colorado Springs, hell, even Vail. It didn't matter where I thought it would happen, but I was sure that my looking at the mountains would cause it to happen. Besides, anything that marked the end of a day back then only caused me more anxiety as I tried to figure out if we could possibly get through another.

Eventually, my psychiatrist got me to a point where I could peek at the sunset. Now, I can actually enjoy it with only a nagging worry in the back of my mind. Still, I don't watch it every night. I mean, why push your luck?

I go to the antique roll-top desk in the corner of the room and raise the cover. There is plenty of stationery and no shortage of ballpoint pens—everything necessary to write a letter to Rebecca. It always seems like a good idea at first, but then I think about how futile an effort it is to spend all that time writing a letter just to tuck it away in a drawer. Before I know it, the pen is back on the desk and the roll-top is down. No sense in writing something that will never be read.

Aunt Beverly knocks just as I close the desk. The door is slightly ajar, so she pokes her head in and quietly says my name.

"Come on in," I reply. She jumps a little. I think she expected me to be asleep and immediately I'm wracked with guilt for scaring her. I rush over to her, apologizing as I go.

"It's okay, dear," she says, placing her hand on my shoulder. She's always trying to comfort me. "I just wanted to bring you a snack. I made some funnel cake."

Only Aunt Beverly. I didn't even know that people actually made funnel cake anywhere except in the back of little trucks at county fairs. In the hand that's not resting on my shoulder is a plate which she raises up to my nose. The sweet aroma registers immediately and is almost an intense enough pleasure to prevent what happens when my eyes take over: pure panic. The funnel cake is covered in white powder. For a brief moment I know that it's powdered sugar, but before long there's no mistaking what it really is: Anthrax.

My eyes, though glazed-over, are fixed on the television screen where the newscaster has said "anthrax" no less than thirty times throughout the broadcast. Before this week, I would have told you it was the name of an old metal band that was named after some obscure, if not extinct, disease. Now, I am brutally aware of what Anthrax is, what it does, and how it can and can't be deployed. Powder in an envelope? Effective.

I glance down at the coffee table where a pile of mail is sealed in an oversized Ziploc bag. No chance I'm touching it. Not until I know it hasn't been contaminated. Rebecca and Andrew walk through the front door, all laughs and giggles. It's only been about a month since the Trade Center collapsed, yet to them it's all fun and games. There have been no more fights at school, which I would like to attribute to my son's classmates coming to their senses, but I'm afraid Andrew has just stopped trying to help. I can't blame him. Saving everyone is a huge burden for such a young boy.

As they approach the living room, the laughs quiet down. They are obviously trying to avoid aggravating me. I can't blame them either, since I've been a little short with them lately. I don't mean to be, but they just refuse to grasp how serious this whole situation is.

"Hi, honey," Rebecca says, apprehensively.

I grunt a reply.

"Where's the mail?" she asks.

I throw my hands up in the air and sigh. "Do you live in a bubble?"

"Excuse me?" she says, glaring at me, her hands firmly planted on her hips.

Andrew looks at his mother, then at me, then silently scampers off down the hallway to his room. He's a smart boy. He'll even do his homework before he plays his video games without us telling him to do so. Looks like tonight that might come in handy.

"Where the hell do you get off talking to me like that?" she yells while somehow still managing to whisper. Either way, the unadulterated anger in her voice captures my attention.

"Becky," I begin.

"Don't you 'Becky' me," she hisses. Apparently, I'm finished here.

"You have been nothing but a miserable son-of-a-bitch for the past month. The news, the papers, the conspiracy theories. We go miles out of our way to avoid bridges and tunnels as much as possible. You stare at every airborne plane like it's going to blow up in front of your eyes. You scare the hell out of our son day in and day out with your so-called lessons. But even with all of that, at the very least you've managed to maintain some common decency. Until tonight."

I look at her in shock, but she avoids looking back at me, as if the very idea sickens her. She probably wouldn't be buying my puppy dog eyes anyway. I think this one's going to take a lot more than that.

"What do you want me to say, Becky?" I ask. It takes me a bit by surprise that I was actually able to get a word in, let alone a whole sentence. Maybe it surprised her, too, because she doesn't answer.

"I'm scared," I continue, seizing the opportunity that she's given me. "I was in one of those buildings. You've seen what they can do, but I *lived* it. I don't know if my mother ever made it out and I probably never will. For the rest of my life I might be wondering just how she died. When. Where."

Rebecca finally turns toward me. She's been leaning on the entertainment center staring at a framed picture of us that was taken in Maine before Andrew was born. It's obviously been collecting dust because the edge over which she's run her finger is shinier than the rest of the frame. She steps away from the picture and walks over to the couch. She looks at me before sitting down, like a person would look at an injured dog that has wandered to their yard: with cautious pity.

There are tears in her eyes. Not enough to overflow and roll down her cheeks, but enough to build on her eyelids and make her eyes glisten. Just a couple of days ago we held my mother's funeral—one of those symbolic things where you bury an empty casket. We were forced to accept the fact that she was lost in the attacks simply because we had no reason to believe otherwise. Hope doesn't count as a reason it seems.

Rebecca places her hand on my stubble-ridden cheek and looks into my eyes. In another moment her forehead is resting against mine and the tips of our noses are touching. I listen to her breathe and hope that it won't be interrupted with words.

It is.

"Jim," she says. It's just one word, but the tone in which she says it gives me a chill. I've heard that tone a hundred times. They use it in the movies: when an elderly man runs into his high school sweetheart after all those years and she finally realizes who he is, that tone is used; when a dead loved one shows up as a ghost or reincarnated in some way, and the surviving loved one realizes what has happened, that tone is used. It's the tone that says, *I know you and I love you, I just couldn't believe that* this *was you.*

"You know that I loved your mother," she continues. "You know how terrible I feel about what happened. I am mourning her just like you are. Andrew is mourning her, too. Terrible things happened that day to many, many people."

I nod, hoping this means she's starting to understand just where I'm coming from. I wait to hear her tell me I've been right all along, that she shouldn't have been upset with me for the way I've been acting, that she will listen to me in regards to this in the future. But what I do hear couldn't be further from that.

"I want you to understand that I get all that. I really do. But you need to understand something else, so listen to me very carefully."

I actually lean in when she says this. I'm not sure what I anticipate her saying, but I wait eagerly.

"Your mother died at Ground Zero, but Andrew and I didn't. We're right here."

The words hit home and, if I wasn't completely distracted by the wallpaper, I don't know how I would respond. The problem isn't that the pattern is a subtle floral pattern; the problem is that we don't have wallpaper. Our walls are painted. The last time I saw wallpaper like that I was at my Aunt Beverly's house …

… which is where I suddenly find myself. My aunt is pressing a cool, damp cloth to my head and repeating in a soothing voice, "It's okay. We're right here."

CHAPTER FIVE

"Clinton, get to steppin' with that water. The Lord will be here for his second go 'round before you are!"

When I fully slip back into the present, I'm lying on my bed staring at the ceiling and Aunt Beverly is calling to Uncle Clint. I try to focus, both visually and mentally, finally mustering enough strength to sit up. Aunt Beverly takes a deep breath when she sees this and lets out a long, powerful exhale.

"I'll get you some water," she assures me, but I wave her off. I don't need water. I don't need anything, really, except maybe a trip back in time to keep the 9/11 attacks from happening in the first place. Besides, I wasn't about to hold my breath waiting for Uncle Clint to do something for his dear ol' nephew.

Once again, I'm proven wrong when Uncle Clint shows up in the doorway with a large glass of ice water. After he hands it off to Aunt Beverly, his hulking figure slouches against the door frame and his squinty eyes peer at me. He thinks I'm a freak, no doubt. I know he got me the water with the utmost contempt, possibly even hoping I'd choke on an ice cube and free up his spare bedroom. I take the glass just to keep him from blowing his top, but I miserably fail at trying to act like I don't want or need the water when I swallow the entire glass in one big gulp. Aunt Beverly shakes her head and admonishes me, insisting that drinking water too fast will kill you.

She strokes my hair and gazes into my eyes with pity. I hate that look. It makes me feel like a three-legged puppy dog. Come to think of it, I kind of smell like one, too. A good shower would come in handy right about now. From the distance she's keeping, I think Aunt Beverly might be thinking the same thing, but is too polite to verbalize it. Out of the corner of my eye, I notice Uncle Clint's figure still hovering in the doorway. I'm not sure if he's genuinely interested in what's going on, or if he's just too lazy to get that mass of flesh and bone moving without a tugboat to help him along.

"Are you okay, dear?" Aunt Beverly asks from out of harm's way.

"Good as always," I say, managing a smile.

"I hoped these were going away," she says.

I smirk. "Yeah, me too. Today's been a little more active than usual. It's just that sometimes weird things trigger it."

"Funnel cake?" she asks, bewildered.

"Kind of. It was the powdered sugar. It made me think of the anthrax attacks that happened about a month after 9/11."

"You ever actually see any anthrax?" she asks.

"No," I reply, and hang my head. "Guess it's not necessary. I just know it's white powder."

"Somethin' that simple?" Uncle Clint mutters.

I don't answer right away, not because I don't want to, but more out of surprise than anything else. There's a tone to his voice that sounds completely alien. If I didn't know better, I'd say it bordered on concern.

"Um, yeah," I manage, trying to make that short, nondescript answer seem sincere. I figure if he can give a little, I can give a little, but my answer is obviously lacking, so I try harder. "Powdered sugar, a knot in wood, the way the sun shines off something, it can be anything. Once the memory starts, I can't stop it. It's almost like I'm actually there and I can't force myself to wake up if I don't realize it's not real."

Silence. Comfortable silence is one of the rarest things on the planet. Either you want to say something, or you want somebody else to say something, or you think they want you to say something, or it's a lonely silence, or a nervous silence. Some people will say that doing something like lying under the stars at night is a comfortable silence, but when you're doing something like that you're so appreciative of your surroundings that you're very aware of the ambient sounds—the crickets, the wind, cars passing on a nearby road. You can't really call that silence. It's only when you want noise that you actually feel silence. Right now, I desperately want somebody to say something.

"I think I'll take a shower," I say when I realize nobody else is going to speak.

I'm bombarded with nervous utterances assuring me that a shower is a good idea, like both my aunt and my uncle have just realized how rude their reactions were. I smile, lips pursed, as they make a quick exit from my room, confident that I am okay.

The sunlight stretches clear across the room now, as the sun approaches the end of its descent above the peaks of the Rockies. Glancing out the window, I reach into my closet and pull my towel off the hook on the back of the door. It's still slightly damp from last night's shower.

I walk barefoot across the hardwood floor of the hallway to the main bathroom. Aunt Beverly and Uncle Clint have one in the master bedroom, so this one is all mine. I shut the door behind me and begin to turn the lock, but I remember my promise to Aunt Beverly that I would never lock myself in a room. She promised to respect my privacy, but wanted to be able to get in to help if I had an episode. I leave the door unlocked, go to the shower and turn the knob to hot. It takes forever for the water to heat up in this house, so I sit on the toilet lid, trying not to think about what's been happening to me. If I think about it, I panic and get anxious. If I get anxious, I'm reminded of my past. If I'm reminded of my past, I flashback. It's a vicious cycle. Minutes later, I notice the mirror fogging up and I step into the shower stall.

The hot water spattering against my skin immediately relaxes my muscles and my breathing calms as the steam opens up my air passages. I take a few deep breaths, then put my head under the water. A moment later, or maybe a lifetime earlier, the door slides open and Rebecca is standing there, looking in.

Oh, not now, I think. She only opens that door for one of two reasons: either she wants to make love or she wants to fight. Unfortunately, I don't think I could perform well in either task right now. And because of that, if she wants the former it will end in the latter.

I look over at her and see she's not wearing anything. I guess that answers my question. I force a smile as she steps into the stall with me.

"Andrew is sound asleep. We've got all night," she whispers, as she wraps her arms around me and nuzzles her head up against my chest. She looks up at me and we hold eye contact. Those eyes are captivating. Unfortunately, captivation isn't necessarily what's needed here. Our lips touch and I do my best to act passionate by letting my hands roam. Despite the fact that I'm a terrible actor, she persists.

We continue to kiss and I thank God that our eyes are now closed, because I'm sure I would crack if I had to look at her. I feel her hands sliding over my body: my shoulders, my back, my chest, my stomach. The whole time I'm praying for a result down below. I try to convince myself to push the image of those towers falling, of the bodies plummeting one hundred stories to the ground, of the fiery plane crashes, out of my mind just long enough to become aroused. If I can just do that, I can avoid the inevitable fight to follow. If I can do that, maybe I can convince my wife that I am not obsessed as she has so frequently called me. If I can do that, maybe I *am* normal.

Then it happens. Her hands slide downward and begin working what I used to think of as their magic, but the magic is really in the sad fact that nothing happens. I give the poor girl credit: she continues to try, she really does, but damn I can't focus. I can't be happy. I just can't.

Eventually, she quits with a huff and I try to hide my sigh of relief. She drops her forehead against my chest for a moment, then leaves without saying a word. I mentally kick myself. I mean, what the hell is wrong with me?

Stupid question. I know exactly what it is. Rebecca knows, too. I turn the water off, reach out the door and grab my towel. After drying off, I wrap the towel around my waist and go into the bedroom where I find Rebecca lying on the bed crying. She makes a poor attempt at hiding the fact that she's crying. So poor, in fact, that it's obvious she wanted me not only to know she was crying, but also to know she was attempting to hide the fact that she was crying. This annoys me a little bit. I mean, come on. Maybe annoyed isn't even strong enough. It makes me flat out angry. If you are feeling something, just say it, right?

"Hey honey, were you crying?" I ask, faux innocent.

"No, no," she says, wiping away the tears. "I just … I just miss you. I miss us."

"What do you mean?" I ask. "I'm here. We're here. Becca?"

She shakes her head, ever so slightly. She knows that I know exactly what she means and my feigned ignorance drives her mad. I want to apologize and plead for her to give me time, but I don't. She's a strong woman. If she's been pushed beyond her breaking point, then no amount of pleading is going to change that.

I sit down next to her on the edge of the bed and rest my head in my hands. She quickly stands up and walks across the room like we're two magnets with the same polarization. The silence and imposed distance is unbearable, but I don't know if I want it to end. I'm afraid of what's waiting on the other side of the void.

Then it comes.

"Andrew and I are going to stay with my mother for a while," she says. She states it as fact. There is no discussion, no debate, no argument to be had.

"What?" I explode. "When the hell did you make this decision?"

"I didn't. You did."

"I ... me? What do you mean?"

"Look, Jim. I'm not a selfish woman. I think you know that. If it was just me, well, I'd deal with your problems. I'd help you work through them for as long as that took, but the fact is, it's not just me. I've got to think about Andrew."

"Andrew is fine."

"You really think so? If you do, you're blind. The boy doesn't know whether to be more scared of leaving the house or coming home to hear more of your stories of terror."

I shake my head. "No, that's not true."

"You don't want to see it. You *won't* see it. That's why we've got to go," she says.

"You don't *have* to do anything. You *want* to do this."

"No, no. No you don't. You don't get to put this back on me," she cries. She's angry now, shaking. I can see that. I mean, I still pretend I can't, but I can.

I want to protest more, but I don't have any ammunition. She's right. Besides, I go into a little bit of shock when she reaches under the bed and slides out the suitcase. I guess the visual drives the reality of this home, but I don't know what hurts more: the sight of the suitcase or the fact it's already packed.

All of a sudden I'm thinking about Andrew. I'm thinking about the huge smile I used to get when I walked through the door after work. I'm thinking about all the nights I stood by the crib and stared in awe at my baby boy. I'm thinking about the hugs and the laughter. I think about all this, and I quickly realize it's all about to come to an end.

Then I think some more and realize it all really ended weeks ago. The smiles, the laughter, and even the hugs—they're gone and it's my fault. Tears are rolling down my cheeks before I even realize I'm crying.

Rebecca stops packing and looks at me. She looks at me like she's never seen me before, but what it must really be is that it's been a long time since she's seen any emotion out of me—other than fear.

"Don't do this. I'm sorry. I'll make it right. Stay and you'll see."

She takes a deep breath and looks me in the eyes. I don't know if she finds what she's looking for there, but whatever she does manage to find doesn't change her mind. She reaches into her drawer and pulls out some underwear. As she slides her panties on up under her towel, she says to me, "No. I'm sorry but no."

"Rebecca," I begin to plead, but she stops me.

"Jim, I'll tell you what. I'll give you your chance. I'll see if we can work this out, but I'm taking Andrew out of the equation. We are moving in with my mother. We are going to stay there for a while. If you can show me that you can get past all this, then we'll see what we can work out. Okay?"

"Okay? You're asking me if taking my son away is okay? No, it's not okay," I holler, before being stopped cold by the stern resolution in her body language. "But I guess it's the best I'm going to get."

She pulls on her jeans. "Yes, it is."

"I guess I should go say goodbye."

"Don't wake him," she says. "I won't rush out of here. I'll load up the car tonight and we'll leave tomorrow. I'll sleep on the couch. In the morning you can say your good-byes."

Suddenly water is running down my face, and I think a pipe must have burst somewhere in my bedroom. When I wipe the water from my eyes and look around, the room is gone and so is Rebecca. The only thing that's left is me in Aunt Beverly's shower. I take my head out from under the cascading water and wonder why my face is still getting wet. Then I let out a sob and allow the stream of tears to keep on coming.

CHAPTER SIX

The sun has set, the temperature has unexpectedly dropped almost thirty degrees, and I can't get out of my towel and into some warm clothes fast enough. The sudden chill has caught us all by surprise. I can tell from the knocking sound rising from the baseboard heaters that Uncle Clint has just turned up the thermostat. Outside, there's a strong wind blowing in from the mountains and it's beating at my window, making the glass rattle in its frame. At times, the rattling gets so violent that I'm positive the glass is about to shatter into a million shards and fly across my room, tearing everything in its path to pieces. For now, though, the window holds.

I sit on the bed and pull the comforter tight around my shoulders as I wait for the room to heat up. The banging is joined by a few clunks and a complimentary clicking noise. There is almost a rhythm to it. When I allow the rattling of the window to join in with the other sounds, it all reminds me of the sound of a train rumbling along the tracks—just like the train that I used to take to and from work every day.

This time, I almost realize that the flashback is coming on. I have a brief moment to panic, but then I'm sitting on a brown vinyl seat staring out through an oblong window, watching buildings and trees speed past. The window rattles slightly as the train car sways from side to side. Everything on the other side of the window is gray—stone-cold gray.

The train is not empty by any means, but it's sparsely occupied compared to the one I used to take. That one leaves the city about an hour later, right in the middle of rush hour. I'm not a morning person, but I make the effort to get out of the house by four o'clock in order to get to Penn Station to catch the second train into Jersey. If a train is going to be a target of terrorism, I would imagine that it's going to be one that has a lot of people on board.

Eventually, I find that I'm no longer looking *through* the window, but rather *at* the window and studying the reflections in the glass. It's still kind of dark outside, so the image of the lit-up car is crisp. I can see most of the other passengers without turning my head: three white males in business suits and one in what appears to be workout clothes, another four African-American males in various types of dress, ranging in age from their early twenties to about sixty, about a half-dozen women both black and white primarily in their thirties. There is nobody of Mid-Eastern descent. There isn't a single turban. Well, at least not in this car.

Outside, the silhouettes of bare trees stretch into the sky like fingers of reanimated skeletons reaching out from their graves in an attempt to rejoin the living. The color of the sky is that of an old, worn headstone. Everywhere I look I see death. I decide that it's time to turn away from the window before I make myself sick to my stomach.

On the seat to my left is a copy of today's *Newark Star Ledger*. I put it there, unopened, when I sat down. I've found it necessary to make some rules in my life, one of which is that I don't read the newspaper before I board the train, otherwise I may never get on. If I never boarded, my job would be gone and, while I could still pay my rent on part time wages somewhere, I couldn't stand the thought of not being able to give Rebecca money to buy things for Andrew.

I still talk to Rebecca every week and to Andrew two or three times that. Each call is supervised, and the moment I head down the path of discussing terrorism, or anthrax, or homeland security, Rebecca interrupts and the call is over. I do my best to stay away from those topics, but it's amazing just how many things lead there.

I pick the newspaper up and unfold it on my lap so that I'm looking at the top half of the front page. I know what I'm going to see. It's December 23rd. Just yesterday they caught a man trying to board a plane with a bomb in his shoe. Unbelievable. Just three days before Christmas and they're still trying to blow things up. Don't these people have any shame? I want to be angrier about this than I am, but I think of Washington's Christmas Eve attack on the British and the Tet Offensive in Viet Nam and I think that maybe surprise attacks on holidays are just an everyday part of warfare. Then I remind myself that this isn't war, this is terrorism: the slaughter of innocents.

I tear the paper open with ferocity as I attempt to get to the meat of the story about the bomber. Richard Reid, blah, blah, blah. British citizen, blah, blah, blah. Claims allegiance to bin Laden. There it is. Not some crazy, homicidal homegrown maniac, but rather a foreign national fighting for bin Laden's cause. Suddenly, I'm looking around the train again and realizing that while I was so concerned about turbans, somebody may have sneaked onto the train with a bomb in their shoe. Of course they wouldn't be wearing a turban. How could I be so stupid? In this day and age, that would just draw attention to them.

I'm nervous. I can't see everybody's shoes. Casually, I try to look around the seats, under the seats, over the seats. It's all I can do to keep from climbing from row to row. I don't know if I expect to see TNT wired in a bundle to the bottom of somebody's foot, but I'm convinced that if there's a bomb in a shoe, I'll see it. My hands are shaking and a cold sweat breaks out in beads on my brow. I know that if I don't get control soon, I'll end up hurting somebody, so I force my butt back into my seat and close my eyes. I inhale through my nose and out through my mouth, repeatedly, trying to focus on something other than the fear. Chinese food. The New York Giants. My favorite television show. Kittens. Hell, anything not terrorist related. After a few moments, my breathing slows and I know it's beginning to work.

I open my eyes and I see that the other people on the train are just commuters like me. Nobody's got a bomb. Nobody's going to kill me. It's all just my paranoid brain making up stories to scare me. I am safe.

Luckily, though, we've arrived at Newark Penn Station, just in case I'm wrong.

My hands are pawing at the doors, trying to tear them open before the train comes to a stop. When they finally part of their own accord, I'm through them and across the platform before I can even take a breath. I might have knocked somebody over in the process, but I'm not sure. I'm running, dodging, and weaving like a pro running back, except I'm not conditioned quite as well. Before I can break out into the open air, a fire ignites in my lungs and I'm forced to stop. My legs begin to fail me, so I lean against the wall and try to take deep breaths.

I remind myself that I am in Newark, not New York. I counter that that doesn't matter: they'll strike anywhere, anytime. I argue that there isn't an Arab as far as the eye can see, but then I tell myself that I'm a fool if I think they're not creative enough to blend in. This internal debate continues on at such a brisk pace that it seems to be keeping step with my heartbeat. I know that I need to calm my thinking in order to calm my heartbeat, so I focus my attention on that.

Chinese food. The New York Giants. My favorite television show. Kittens. I need some new distractions. These never seem to work. I look around the train station and start to read things: signs, newspaper or magazine headlines, arrival and departure times, pretty much anything that will hold my attention for one or two seconds. Luckily, this seems to work. I start reading logos on sweatshirts and jackets and within a few minutes my breathing and heart rate seem to return to normal. I take one final deep breath, and even though it feels shallow, like when you try to take a deep breath after being in the ocean all day, it is still relieving.

I gasp for one more and when I get it, it comes much easier. Too easy, in fact. Something doesn't feel right. I look around, then let out a sigh that's a mix of relief and frustration as I realize that I'm in Aunt Beverly's house. I was worried I'd had another panic attack, but instead it was another flashback. I close my eyes. There is nothing I want to do more, right now, than sleep, but my overactive brain isn't going to let that happen.

CHAPTER SEVEN

The wind is no longer rattling my window, but I can still hear it whistling across the fields outside, whipping plants and grasses back and forth with a swooshing sound that reminds me of hundreds of people skiing in synchronicity. As soon as I realize that the sound reminds me of something, I stiffen up, expecting to be pulled deep into another flashback, but I quickly and thankfully discover I have no terrorist memories connected with skiing.

I've been lying awake in bed for a couple of hours now. At least I think I've been lying awake. Every once in a while I glance at the glowing numbers on my digital alarm clock and notice that minutes have passed more quickly than they could have possibly passed if I truly had been awake. So, most likely I've taken a catnap here or there.

The house is silent, with the exception of the occasional knocking of the baseboard heaters and a random, unidentified creak here and there. The heat is doing its job a little too well and I'm forced to fling the flannel sheets, fleece blanket, and patchwork quilt that were all necessary just a few short hours ago, from my body and lift my t-shirt to cool off a bit.

After a few minutes of tossing around and fanning myself, the discomfort is more than I can bear. I swing my feet off the mattress and place them on the floor. Just the cool feeling of the hardwood on the soles of my feet is enough to relax me a little bit. I get up and pad across the room, out into the hallway, and toward the kitchen where I forage through the refrigerator trying to find something to drink. There isn't a great selection. It's pretty much milk or water, so I take out a gallon of milk and pour myself a glass.

I head into the den where I throw myself onto the sofa in front of the television set. Groping blindly in the dark, I discover the remote control wedged between two couch cushions, free it from its captivity, and press the power button. The glow of the screen gradually increases until the room is bathed in an eerie blue. The light from the screen allows me to better operate the remote, which I use to scroll through the endless infomercials that are broadcast at this time of night. By about channel three hundred and something (Aunt Beverly and Uncle Clint may be farmers, but they are no strangers to the pleasures of satellite television) I find an old movie. Well, it's old to me, but it was probably made in the 1980's. I think I saw it in the theaters when I was a teenager. I don't remember much about it other than the fact that there is a nerdy kid who is continually picked on by the popular crowd. At the end, I think he has his last laugh somehow, but I guess I'll find out.

I'm watching the movie in a daze, images and sounds dancing across my eyes and ears, but only occasionally drilling down into my brain where I can make sense of any of them. Then one sound catches my attention: laughter. It's not just any type of laughter, but a really specific kind: the kind that cannot be mistaken for joyous laughter or hysterical laughter. It is a kind that is immediately recognizable as a demeaning, mocking laughter. I shudder, unsure of why that sound produces such a chill. Then I realize it's because I've heard it before.

It wasn't when I was a child. I'm not proud to say it, but I was more often a *mocker* when I was a kid, not a *mockee*. No, it was from when I was an adult and not too long ago at that. It was post-9/11.

I can hear the laughter very distinctly and it's obvious that it is no longer coming from a movie. In fact, the very idea that I was watching a movie quickly fades away as the New York City street comes into view before me. There is a row of restaurants and bars on my right, most with outdoor seating areas that are closed for the winter. Now they are a gathering spot for smokers who are taking advantage of a fairly mild winter's night to get some fresh air, as oxymoronic as that might seem.

I spent a late night at the office, poring over message boards and news groups to keep up with the latest on Al Qaeda, bin Laden, and the troops in Afghanistan. Now, making my way home, I'm so tired I can hardly lift my feet off the ground and a throbbing headache has developed behind my eyes. My stomach growls and I realize I haven't had anything to eat since a Danish sometime around nine-thirty this morning. I continue like a zombie that has no purpose but to drag itself onward until it finds nourishment.

As I pass each bar, I glance up at the sign and consider heading inside for some food and a beer, but it all seems like so much effort. I'll keep on going until I find a fast food restaurant or a Chinese takeout. As I near the corner, I hear some familiar voices. This is where that laughter was coming from. I look up to find Jeff smoking with a group of our other co-workers that commute from the city. Happy to see them, I begin to head their way before realizing that they seem to be out celebrating a happy hour to which I wasn't invited. Jeff sees that I've spotted them, and his eyes immediately go to the ground at his feet. The others don't look away. I guess they don't feel as guilty as Jeff does for not inviting me. I decide to be the bigger man and approach the group with a smile.

"Hey guys," I say with enthusiasm.

Richard, one of the salesmen and one of the loudest people I have ever met, offers his greeting first. "Hey Jim, how are you buddy? We were just talking about you."

A few members of the group snicker as Tom runs his hand back through his thick mane of hair. Each strand falls perfectly back into place as he flashes that so-called charming smile that melts our potential customers. I think about the mocking laughter I heard before I approached and have a lot of trouble keeping a smile on my face. Jeff still won't raise his eyes to meet mine.

"Really?" I ask, directing it at my supposed best friend.

"Sure," Richard responds, obviously confident that everybody is enjoying their little inside joke. "We were just saying how good a job you're doing at the office."

One guy in the back lets out a little chuckle with such a burst of air that it sounds like someone punched him in the gut. Charlie, our accountant, shoves his hands in his pockets and lets out a deep breath, obviously uncomfortable. Jeff looks up, finds me looking right back at him and quickly turns away.

"What do you mean, Richard?"

"Well, who would keep us safe in our office if you weren't hunting down all those conspiracy theories all day long?"

More laughter. Jeff makes a feeble attempt to ask Richard to stop, but for a moment I'm almost positive I caught a smile on the corners of his mouth. Rage begins to build inside me. Fools. Each and every one of them is a fool.

I look at each face in the group, shake my head in disgust and walk away. I try to put on an air of superiority, but inside my gut is wrenching from fury and embarrassment. There isn't a person in that crowd I wouldn't have called a friend ten minutes ago.

As I walk away, I keep hoping that Jeff will come chasing after me and invite me back to the bar where I end up receiving a big apology from everyone. In that fantasy, not only do they realize that they are wrong for their condescending behavior, but they also realize the inherent value in my concern for what is happening to our country.

But Jeff never comes. In fact, I'm pretty sure I heard his laugh among the mockery that continued after I left. Right now I hate him. I hate them all. My embarrassment, ire and aggression are all focused on my co-workers until two figures near a bus stop catch my eye. I don't know the bus schedule for this route, but I don't see anybody waiting except these two men. They're talking quietly to one another in what I feel to be a suspicious manner. Maybe it's the way they lean into one another when they speak or maybe it's the fact that they just seem to be keeping to the shadows, but I don't like what I'm seeing.

I've heard stories about people who ran into the 9/11 hijackers in the airport before takeoff or in the hotel the night before, but lacked the vigilance and foresight to recognize an imminent threat. I am determined to never be one of those people.

Without looking directly at the two men, I move myself into a position where I can see their faces, though they're not necessarily looking in my direction. Now I know why they caught my eye: they are both Middle-Eastern. I focus every drop of malice from my earlier encounter on these two men. That laughter that is eating away at me, in my mind, came from these two men instead of my co-workers. I know what they must be up to and I hate them for it.

I skulk around the sidewalk and am awestruck by the fact that, aside from myself, not one other single person is paying the slightest bit of attention to these two obvious terrorists. Why haven't the police stopped to question these two? Why aren't other pedestrians raising an alarm? Do they really think that any bus driver in his right mind is going to let them board?

The two Arabs continue their quiet conversation, boldly dismissing everybody that walks by. I can't believe their arrogance! Do they think that Americans are so ready to let this happen to us again? Do they think that we don't have our eyes on them?

Stepping back for a moment and assessing my situation, I figure that by now I'm probably beginning to look a little suspicious myself, so I look around for a place that I can go or something that I can do that will still allow me to keep tabs on them. Unfortunately, when I glance down the street I see my co-workers headed my way. Happy hour must have finally ended. Weighing my options, I decide that some garbage cans in front of the nearest shop are going to have to provide sufficient cover. I dive down, hoping that it was quick enough to avoid detection.

Richard and posse draw nearer as I hold my breath, trying to split my attention between them and the all-too-obvious terrorists at the bus stop. Still no bus. How stupid do they think we are? Now, my co-workers, who are practically on top of me, should notice the two men. Anticipation of vindication pervades my being. When they notice the terrorists, they'll realize just how right I've been all along, but God, if it's possible they could still be ignorant when the truth is laid out before their eyes, please just let them continue on. Please.

Richard stops just a few feet away and I'm pretty sure it's no coincidence. A few vestiges of hope remain that they might see what I see, but without a word, he reaches down and yanks me up by my collar. I feel like a school boy caught peeping into the girls' locker room by the headmaster. I can feel my cheeks flush with heat and I'm sure I'm a nice crimson color by now, though the neon from the signs in the window probably helps to conceal that. I can't look any of my so-called friends in the eyes, but I can hear their laughter all too clearly.

"What are you doing?" Richard asks, with genuine awe in his voice.

I want to quiet him, but don't know how. *Shh!* is probably not going to do the trick. I glance to the two figures at the bus stop and the moment I do, I realize only more torment can follow. Richard follows my gaze, which gives me the opportunity to look back at my co-workers. Jeff is not with them. Thank God for that.

"Are you spying on them?" Richard asks, his voice booming, his finger pointing directly at the terrorists.

Just when I thought I couldn't be any more embarrassed, Richard helped me get over that obstacle. Thanks, Richard. Without turning my head, I know the two men at the bus stop are now looking at us. Damn this asshole. Now they know I was on to them. Either he just signed our death warrant or they'll cancel their plans and attack another city on another day. More lives will be lost regardless of which scenario plays out.

"You've got some serious problems," Richard says, making me wish, at this point, that one of his cohorts would take over the belittling and berating. I'm just all charmed out.

"I don't have problems," I stammer, trying to gain some confidence, which is a lot like trying to climb up the descending track of a roller coaster just as a string of cars crests the peak. I can even picture Richard sitting in the foremost car.

"What the hell do you call this, then?" Richard asks, gesturing toward the two men. "Hiding in garbage cans so you can spy on people isn't a problem?"

"I wasn't hiding in there to spy on them," I say, realizing too late that I should have left it alone. Now, I'll have to explain that I was actually hiding from *him*.

Surprisingly, Richard spares me the discomfort and doesn't ask what I mean. Instead, he just shakes his head and laughs. He finally releases my collar and, though I feel the urge to sprint away as fast as I possibly can, my feet remain planted on the concrete.

"So what is it you think they're doing?" Richard asks. He almost sounds half-sincere.

I contemplate simply ignoring him, but deep inside I know the only reason I haven't yet run away is because I was hoping for the chance to justify my actions. That chance was just given to me, so I need to take it.

"Can't you see?" I ask, hoping that one simple question will make it all clear. When no looks of sudden comprehension appear on their faces, I go on.

"They're terrorists, exchanging information. Look," I say, pointing directly at the two men. By this point I've lost any concern about whether they see us or not, and obviously they've lost any concern with us because they're no longer looking our way.

"Two Middle-Eastern men, standing at a bus stop at night, whisper-ing to each other, sticking to the shadows. What else could it possibly be?"

Richard has a serious deep-thinking look on his face. He nods. "Maybe you're right," he says. I feel a warmth course through my body. I feel like I can hold my chin up higher.

"What else could it be?" Richard asks, rhetorically. "Hm. Terrorists, huh?"

I nod enthusiastically, like a cartoon puppy that's just been offered a treat. You can almost hear the cheesy *dink-dink-dink* sound effect.

"Well, I guess there's only one way to find out, don't you think?"

I'm not sure where he's going with this, but suddenly I don't like it at all.

"Hey Neeraj," he calls out, before I can beg him to be quiet. At first, it doesn't even strike me as strange that he calls the man by name.

"What's up, Rich?" the shorter of the two men calls back. My gut is sinking again, this time to the point where I want to retch all over my shoes. The guy doesn't even have an accent.

"Where ya headed?"

"Up to Hartford. We've got a conference there for the rest of the week."

"Have fun. Need me to take in your mail?"

Richard looks at me with disgust as he continues this friendly ban-ter.

"No, thanks. My sister is going to be coming by to feed the cat so she'll take it in."

Oh, Christ. As if it wasn't bad enough, the son-of-a-bitch has a cat. No self-respecting terrorist would own a cat.

The bus that the two men had apparently been waiting for pulls to the curb and opens its doors with a hiss. Neeraj and friend grab their bags that were leaning against the far side of the bus stop and wave to Richard before boarding the bus. After it pulls away, Richard glares at me.

"They're Indians, moron," are the only words he says, or needs to say, as he walks away.

His entourage follows, some cackling, some giggling, some chuckling, but all doing so with intense mockery. I cover my ears because I can't take anymore. I close my eyes hoping that this whole world will just go away.

To my surprise, it does. When I open my eyes, I am staring at a television screen which is running the closing credits of a movie with some goofy Eighties song playing over them. I've missed the entire thing. I guess I'll never find out how that boy gets his last laugh after all.

CHAPTER EIGHT

When I finally peel my near-comatose butt off the couch, *Good Morning America* is broadcasting some human interest story about a Midwestern family that's about to have their umpteenth kid. I quietly growl obscenities at the television, pronouncing the infinite stupidity of this family while simultaneously cursing their happiness. I'm grouchy because I'm tired. I'm tired because I've gotten absolutely no sleep and the way these flashbacks are kicking in, I don't see any in my near future. Sure, I'm damn near unconscious when I have one of my episodes, but they're anything but refreshing.

I throw my arms in the air and stretch with a loud groan that either comes from my throat or from one of my joints, but it doesn't sound good, regardless. When I drop my arms, a series of loud cracks and pops emanate from my back. Even though it sounds like my body is falling to pieces, it all feels great.

Through the slats of the Venetian blinds I can see that everything outside is frost-covered. Right now, that does nothing more than make me want to slide into bed, pull up my comforter and close my eyes, whether sleep comes or not. I've already placed my bet on which it will be.

I creep down the hallway, trying my best to keep the boards from squeaking. It's not that Aunt Beverly and Uncle Clint would mind that I was up all night, but the moment my aunt wakes up she'll be fawning all over me and won't give me a chance to enjoy the comfort of my bed. Luckily, there are only soft, rumbling snoring noises coming from their room.

Still asleep.

Good.

I tiptoe into my room and get into the unmade bed. The covers are where I left them when I threw them off me last night, so the mattress and sheets are ice-cold. I crawl in, pull the covers up to my chin, and wait for my body heat to warm them up. It doesn't take long, but despite the comfort (and as predicted) sleep doesn't come. I'm relaxed, though, which is probably the first time in the last twenty-four hours. It's been an unusually bad day.

By last count, I've had precisely a whole lot of flashbacks and that's just a whole lot too many. I've relived these moments over and over (and over) for the past few years but never in such rapid succession. The blackouts have come along maybe once every few days, but since yesterday morning they've been once every few minutes.

I don't pretend to be the only person in the world who tortures himself by repeatedly playing past mistakes in his mind. Many people have disastrous moments they look back on in an attempt to determine what they could have done differently. Problem is: I've got a whole series of them.

I don't flash back to the nights spent with my son and wife in front of the Christmas tree, carols playing in the background. I don't flash back to days spent in the park enjoying the summer air and watching my boy chase butterflies. I don't flash back to our wedding day, Andrew's birthday, or anything good. Sure, I remember those days— the memories are the only things that keep me going most of the time—but I don't flash back. The flashbacks are all of things I wish I could change.

Oh, and I can't control them. I've tried. I've tried to stop them and when that seemed futile, I tried to focus them on the good memories. Nothing worked. Meditation, hypnosis, voodoo: nothing.

Besides, voodoo dolls and shrunken heads? *Very* hard to explain.

The bed is very warm now and it feels great. I adjust the comforter under my chin, try to get comfortable, then roll over onto my side. I grab the waistband of my sweatpants and twist so that they're properly oriented with my boxers and my body, then I do the same with the legs. I fix my t-shirt, too. When I'm done fidgeting, I find myself staring at the telephone.

All I need to do is pick it up and dial ten little numbers, eleven if you count the one for long distance. Eleven little numbers and I can hear Andrew's voice. It's been so long I'm not sure I'd recognize it. Maybe he's hitting puberty and his voice is changing. I mean, what kind of father doesn't even know if his son has hit puberty yet?

Unfortunately, even if I actually had those eleven little numbers and somebody on the other end answered, they would hang up as soon as they heard my voice. Even if it wasn't God-awful early, Rebecca wouldn't allow me to speak to Andrew. She used to screen the calls, but eventually she became ambitious, moved to the opposite coast, and got an unlisted number. After that, I started to wonder if maybe she didn't want me calling her.

As my thoughts continue to wander, sleep begins to hover over me. I can feel it weighing down on my chest and dragging my eyelids closed. My legs ache. I just want sweet, peaceful sleep. Before I finish drifting away, my eyes focus on the picture next to the phone. It's a family portrait and all three of us look so happy. With my thumb, I absent-mindedly finger the gold band on my left ring finger. I've never once removed it. At this point, I don't think I could without the aid of a blowtorch.

The fog of sleep continues to nestle itself around my senses, numbing me to all external stimulation. It plays games with my mind, making me hear or see things that aren't necessarily there. I'm ready to let myself go, to completely relax, when there is a soft tapping at the door. For a moment, my thoughts go to Andrew. In my heart, I know it's my little boy asking to come in and snuggle between his mommy and his daddy on an unusually chilly autumn morning. I try desperately to convince myself of this, but my mind rejects the idea. Stupid mind. Maybe it's actually protecting me, though—shielding me from the pain I'd feel when I discovered that not only was my son not on the other side of that door, but he wasn't even in the same state.

I try, in the haze of sleep, to make myself believe that it's Rebecca, but not only does my mind reject this idea, it actually laughs at it and threatens my heart that if it ever attempts anything so foolish again, it will excommunicate it from my body. When all of this back and forth is over, I decide to open my eyes and accept the fact that it's Aunt Beverly checking up on me.

My vision finally comes into focus and I see my aunt poking her head through the door, though something about her looks different. I can't tell if it's the skin or the eyes or the hair, but it is definitely something. I reach up and rub my eyes which feel laden with ten or twelve hours of sleep, rather than the few minutes of rest I actually got. Then it dawns on me what it is about Aunt Beverly that's different. It's the skin, the eyes *and* the hair.

The skin is smoother around the eyes and at the corners of the mouth. Her hair has significantly fewer gray strands streaking through it. The combination of those two differences takes quite a few years off her appearance, but her bloodshot eyes and the dark, puffy bags underneath add those years back on.

She looks like she's been crying. Even though I know she occasionally cries for me, this looks like long term, intense, emotional crying. This crying is one of loss, a loss that will wrinkle and gray her over the next few years. This crying is over her sister and I suddenly realize that it's not years after 9/11, it's months. In fact, just yesterday, the family gathered at Aunt Beverly's house for the reading of my mother's will. Mom had some money, not that it does her any good now.

I glance around the room and for a second I realize that this room, this bed, will be mine once I've made myself completely incapable of functioning on my own, but before the thought can finish, I've forgotten my future. Strange concept, but that's exactly what I do each time I slip into one of these flashbacks, I forget my future.

Aunt Beverly gives me one of the most painful smiles I have ever seen and asks if I'm hungry for some breakfast. While she waits for my answer, I can tell she is holding back tears. She manages to keep her eyes dry, but she's not quite as successful in keeping her lower lip from quivering.

"You shouldn't bother yourself with breakfast. We'll all be fine on our own," I say, knowing perfectly well that the idea of not personally serving her guests three square meals a day is an idea that would horrify her even if she were a quadriplegic.

She pushes the door open and places her fists on her hips. "You must be mad with grief," she says, but we both know that that statement more accurately describes her. "Now get in that kitchen ...," she begins, but she can't finish. Her voice becomes feeble and she lets out a pathetic whimper. The fists shoot up from her hips to cover her eyes. She's still too proud to admit she's crying.

Uncle Clint comes down the hallway and stops behind Aunt Beverly. "You okay?" he asks, without even glancing in at me. He hasn't said more than two words to me since I alienated my wife and son. He blames me, but he doesn't realize I was just trying to protect them. Some people are very pig-headed.

"Leave me be, Clinton," she manages between a couple of shallow sobs. "Go brew some coffee for our guests. They'll all be up soon."

Without question, he continues on down the hallway. Once he's out of earshot, Aunt Beverly lets go. She quickly moves into the room and shuts the door behind her to hide her emotions from anybody else that might happen by.

"Sit down," I say, patting the mattress. It's not so much a desire to offer her comfort as it is a fear she'll fall and crack her head open and her pride won't allow me to call for help.

Now seated on the bed, she cries for almost five minutes straight. I don't interrupt her. There comes a point where you just need to get it all out and getting cut short can only make things worse. I wait patiently, but I can't keep my mind focused on what she's going through. I still have the vision of an airplane smashing into the World Trade Center etched into my mind. I can still feel the building shake if I focus. I still try to put myself in the shoes of those poor people aboard Flight 93 and debate over whether or not I would have possessed the same amount of courage. I think about anthrax and shoe bombers. I think about the Pentagon and the smoke filled streets of lower Manhattan. I think about the possibility that the George Washington Bridge and the Lincoln Tunnel will most likely be destroyed in the near future. I think about all this and I completely forget about my mother's sister.

When she finishes crying she takes a few deep breaths and pulls a tissue from the pocket of her house dress. From the looks of it, it's been used before, but she doesn't hesitate to dab her eyes with it and blow her nose.

"I'm so sorry," she finally says. "I didn't mean to burden you. You have enough to worry about."

"You didn't burden me, you cried," I say, finally able to concentrate enough to make an attempt at condolence. "There's nothing wrong with that."

"There is. I should be strong. You've lost your mother and …," she says, trailing off again. This time, though, it's not because she's crying. It's because she feels awkward.

"It's okay," I say. "Because I've lost my wife and son. You can say it."

It's become much easier for me to say, but only because I do everything I can to dissociate the words from their meanings. I can't help but wonder if it went unnoticed that I didn't use their names. If I say my son and wife, I can pretend that I'm someone else, maybe an actor in a role or maybe some poor stranger half a world away that I'll never meet. I can trick my mind into believing these things as long as I don't say their names. If I happen to even think about their names, I fall apart.

Aunt Beverly grasps my hand in hers. "How are you doing, dear?" she asks.

I would try to fool her into believing I'm fine, but I'm not half the actor that she is and frankly, she sucks. I shake my head to indicate that I'm not doing well.

She rubs my head and I suddenly feel the most comfortable I've felt since I was in grade school. The look she is giving me and the way she strokes my hair like I'm a beloved pet about to be put to sleep is exactly how my mother would treat me whenever I failed a test, got cut from a sports team, or struck out with the girls. For the first time I realize just how similar my mother and her sister are ... were. If I close my eyes and listen to Aunt Beverly speak, then my mother will be here in this very room, talking to me.

Aunt Beverly/Mom goes on to assure me that everything will be okay and that everything happens for a reason. She tells me how my wife and I will be back together and how I have to trust in the Lord. She tells me that these things just take time and that we're all going through a tough stage in our lives. She tells me all this, but I'm not listening to the words. I'm listening to the sound of her voice.

Each word is stressed the way my mother would stress it. The inflection is my mother to a "T." At one point, I hear her say, "You know what's ironic?" and something makes me pay attention. "After hitting it big on those computer stocks, your mother was so paranoid that family she had never met before would be crawling out of the woodwork to get a piece of the pie. She spent months alienating herself from family she *did* know to keep them from taking advantage of her. She gave up many of the people she loved because of money."

I want to ask why that's ironic, but I don't get the chance. "Don't you see?" she continues, "All that time was wasted and now that she's gone, she's giving those same people all of her money."

I'm afraid to respond to anything she says, right or wrong, superfluous or poignant, because then she might stop talking and my mother will once again be gone, buried beneath one hundred and ten floors of rubble. My mother will no longer be in this room and that tears at my heart because for the first time since the attacks I know where she is.

I pull my knees up to my chest and drop my face into my hands. *Just don't stop talking*, I think, *don't ever stop talking*. But eventually, of course, she does. She stops talking and just watches me. The silence is nerve-wracking and suddenly I find myself hoping she hasn't asked me a question because there's no way to hide the fact that I haven't been listening to a word she's said.

I'm about to speak, about to utter some nonsense or other when she breaks the silence for me. "You look like her, you know. You look just like your mother, but, more importantly, you have her gentle demeanor. Don't ever change that. It is a wonderful trait of your mother's that you can make immortal. If there is one aspect of her personality that influences your life, let it be her gentle kindness."

She rises from the bed and appears to stand a bit more upright than when she first entered the room. Her eyes no longer look on the verge of producing a sudden deluge. Even her breathing seems easier. I guess all she needed was for somebody to listen. So I did and now she's almost a different person. Where does that leave me? How come I can't heal like that? How come I can't stop …

But I can stop. For the past ten minutes, ever since I realized the similarity between her voice and my mother's, the events of 9/11 didn't cross my mind once. In talking to me, she seemed to rid herself of her grief, but she also helped to rid me of my fears, if only temporarily. I take a deep breath and tell myself that there is somewhere on this planet that I can feel comfortable, somewhere where I can escape the terrors of modern life. I smile and my cheeks hurt because the smile muscles have probably atrophied.

Aunt Beverly heads out into the hallway, gives me a quick smile over her shoulder, and informs me that I'd better be at that breakfast table in five minutes if I know what's good for me. I nod and assure her that there's no way I'd miss it. It feels great to not worry, but it isn't long before the thoughts start to return, slowly at first then faster, screaming and yelling and kicking and flailing, like dozens of rowdy kids returning to the pool after the end of adult swim has been announced. I cover my ears and close my eyes, knowing that it won't help but hoping for a miracle. When I open my eyes again, I can feel something different. I feel a few years older and a bit more removed from my mother's death. I know if I saw Aunt Beverly now, she'd be more worn-down. Her tears, anger, and grief would be long-past. All of this points to one indisputable truth: I've returned.

CHAPTER NINE

I rise from bed and notice, not surprisingly, that the sun is at a high angle. It must be approaching noon, which makes another wasted morning. I'm sure Uncle Clint will let me know in no uncertain terms how much he appreciates that. I stop myself before walking out into the hallway, figuring I should probably at least change my clothes. I grab a balled-up pair of jeans and a t-shirt from one of the dresser drawers and put them on. The reflection in the mirror still looks like that of a man who's wearing the clothes he slept in. Oh well.

The chill of last night has gone and the windows in my room have been opened to let in a more seasonal breeze. I don't feel at all uncomfortable walking around barefoot and wearing jeans and just a t-shirt. The cool floor actually feels good on the soles of my feet. Exiting my room and walking down the hall, I notice that my head is heavy with lingering sleep. I release a huge yawn as I pass the hallway mirror and notice that my mouth does this thing that makes me look like an elephant chewing a trunkful of grass.

Rubbing my eyes and getting a slight chuckle from the way I look, I stumble into the kitchen where Uncle Clint is on the phone having a hushed conversation. He looks at me in surprise, as if he expected that I would never rise from my slumber, and turns away. Speaking more clearly than he had been before I entered the room, he says, "Okay, then. Let me get going. It was good to talk to you. I will call you again soon."

Phony, I think. Putting on a show. Immediately my mind wanders to the dark recesses of suspicion, wondering just what it is Uncle Clint is trying to hide. I make an attempt to conceal my disdain, but I find myself trying to pierce his heart with my stare. He clicks the power button on the cordless phone and stares out the window for a moment—a long moment.

Finally he turns, but by this time I have peeled my eyes off him and made my way into the refrigerator to find some breakfast-like lunch food, like pizza or an old egg roll, but of course Aunt Beverly wouldn't be caught dead with something like that in her house. In fact, since she actually never lets either Uncle Clint or myself leave the table until all the food she's cooked is gone, there is *nothing* already prepared in the refrigerator. I grab a hunk of cheese from the produce drawer and remove some of the plastic wrap to take a sniff. I like American cheese—good old homegrown, one-hundred percent processed cheese that comes in individual pieces of plastic. Uncle Clint eats stuff that stinks. Fortunately, this hunk falls somewhere in between.

I close the refrigerator doors to find Uncle Clint still standing there, seemingly lost. My plan this morning had been to make an attempt to be nice to him, but after catching the tail end of that sneaky phone call, I'm not so sure I want to do that.

"You okay?" I ask. I move to the stove, realize that I still need butter to make my grilled cheese sandwiches, and go back to retrieve some.

"Yeah," he says. I decide, at that moment, to nickname him Uncle Eloquence.

"Just an old friend," he says, nodding at the phone and answering a question I didn't ask. He gives this answer with more guilt than a guy who just stole his best friend's kitten as a last minute gift to give to his girlfriend because he forgot their anniversary. Okay, just trust me on that one: guilt out the wazoo.

"Old friend," I mutter, turning to the stove. I pull a pan off the overhead rack and set it on the burner. I butter the bread and slice the cheese—*obvious* signs that I don't believe a word he's said.

"Yeah," he says, gaining some confidence. "High school. Just moved back to town. Wants to catch up."

He heads over to the other side of the room where he places the phone in its cradle to charge. I can see right through him. I know there's no way Uncle Clint ever had any friends, not even in high school that sleazy bastard. I could choke him right here and now for what he's doing to Aunt Beverly.

He turns and looks at me like he's about to say something. My back is to him while I cook away, but I can feel him looking at me. I hear him draw breath, but the words don't come right away. He seems to be contemplating something.

"Just before my friend called," he says, "I got a weird call. Somebody was asking if you lived here, but he wouldn't say who it was."

"And?" I ask. The one word is all I can manage without my voice cracking. I use my body to block his view of my hands. They are shaking so hard I have to put the knife down to avoid injuring myself.

"I told him I don't answer questions for people who aren't willing to identify themselves. Then I hung up." He paused, probably to give me time to offer some information, but I remain silent.

"You know who it might have been?"

I shake my head and try to appear unconcerned.

He utters an unsatisfied grunt, then all I hear are footsteps followed by the screen door opening and slamming shut.

That door slamming shut. The sound sends me reeling back a few years. Of course, I'm the last one to leave after the reading of the will. Everyone else stayed long enough to hear what they were or weren't getting, give me a pat on the head, and hop into their minivans (all except my cousin Greg who had already purchased a brand new Ford Mustang convertible in anticipation of his healthy windfall). Now, with everyone gone, I trail my green army-issue canvas sack behind me (though I didn't get mine from the army so much as I got it from the army-navy store) as I shuffle across the porch and down the front steps. That's when the door slams and I stop in my tracks. The sound is so final.

I can't convince my feet to continue on toward the car. I know that if I leave, I might not return. Back in that big, bad city—back in New York—there is so much death, so much destruction. Hell, who knows what buildings or bridges were destroyed while I was gone. We no longer have just bin Laden to worry about, now it's the Axis of Evil: Iraq, Iran, and North Korea. All of them are either stockpiling WMD's (that's weapons of mass destruction to the lay people) or developing their nuclear programs. The world is going to hell, but at least out here I can pretend like I'm not a part of that world.

A few minutes later, I hear the door squeak open again, followed by footsteps on the wooden planks of the porch and stairs. Aunt Beverly's shadow reaches me before she does, but even that is comforting. She comes up next to me and interlocks her arm with mine.

"You all right?" she whispers, her voice hushed even further by the faint breeze.

Good ol' Aunt Beverly, always looking out for me, trying to save me a little embarrassment. She looks up at me with my mother's eyes and I see an ocean of sorrow. I don't think she wants me to leave. Maybe I remind her of my mother, too.

"I'm okay," I reply. "I guess I'm just not looking forward to the long trip back."

"Your mother left you quite a bit. Why don't you fly back. You can drop the car off at the air-," she stops abruptly, and purses her lips. I don't think I gave her a look, so I must have trembled. Something must have betrayed my fears.

"I'm sorry," she says. "You still won't fly?"

I shake my head but don't bother speaking any words. I can't find many, these days, that really express what I'm feeling. Looking down at the ground, I trace little circles in the dirt with my sneaker, waiting for

Aunt Beverly to say something else. Until she does, I'm stuck. I can't head to the car without being rude and right now I just can't seem to speak, so here I stand, waiting.

"You know, Jim," she says, taking a step away from the house, "you don't have to leave." She tugs at my arm and my feet begin to match hers, step by step. She doesn't say anything further, so I guess it's my turn.

"I don't know."

Genius. That's all I can come up with. Not, "Oh what a fantastic idea, I could use the change of pace," and not, "I think it would improve my life greatly right now to get out of the city," and not even, "Really? Thank you." No, I come up with, "I don't know." I want to smack myself in the forehead, but somehow I manage to keep my hand in check.

"Well, it's just a thought. If you change your mind, we are always here for you. We're your family."

We circle past the barn on our little stroll and out toward the pond. It's frozen over and surrounded by yellowed grass that's covered with random patches of snow. Everything is dead.

"I know you are," I say, intentionally leaving Uncle Clint out of my consideration. "I do have to go, though. I've got a job to return to and, well, to be honest, I can't be this far away from Andrew. Not now. Not yet."

She pats my hand. "I understand," she whispers.

That's good, I think, because I don't.

We continue our walk in silence, circling the pond, then back up around the barn and to the rental car. I pick up my bag on the way and drop it with a crunch on a patch of frozen grass. I turn to Aunt Beverly and give her a hug. It is a strong, loving hug that, in my mind, says, *Don't listen to me. Make me stay. Tell me I can't leave. Knock me out if you have to, but don't believe this line of crap that I'm feeding you. I love it here. It comforts me. I can relax, and breathe, and live. I can't do that back home, not anymore. Not since they took my life away from me. Please, I'm begging you, don't let me leave. I won't survive.*

When I release Aunt Beverly from my embrace, I scan her face to see if the hug told her anything, but unfortunately her ESP is not so sharp these days. Curse her for not reading my mind. What does she expect me to do—tell her how I feel? Does she think this is easy?

I give her another moment, but when the silence becomes awkward, I open the door of the car and throw my bag across to the passenger's seat. I throw it a little harder than I intended and I hope that my aunt doesn't sense my hostility. I know it's not rational to be angry with her, but unfortunately rationale has not been in charge of my decision making lately.

"I'd better get going," I say. "Traffic's not going to get any lighter and I want to make as much of the trip as I can before I have to shack up at a motel somewhere."

"I understand," she says, managing a smile.

"Thanks again for everything." I slide into the car and turn the key. The ignition turns over with a gentle roar before I look back over my shoulder and assure my aunt I will see her soon. I don't ask her to say good-bye to Uncle Clint for me. She knows there's no love lost between us and while that hurts her a little bit, she does understand why we're not exactly compatible.

I slam the door shut, roll down the window, and stick my arm out to wave as I drive away. I'm still a bit angry, so I hit the gas a little harder than I would have liked. A high-pitched squeal erupts from the tires as they kick a cloud of dust into the air. My car lurches forward, but not before the dust pushes its way in through my open window.

I'm speeding away from the farm, partially blinded and trying desperately to make out some images through the cloud of dust, but when I do, they turn out to be a stove, a refrigerator, and some pots and pans. The dust cloud is no longer dust, but rather a huge puff of smoke.

It takes me a second to finally realize where I am and what's going on. I'm back at Aunt Beverly's house cooking some lunch, which, by the look of things, is not going to be edible. I reach down, turn off the burner, remove the pan from the heat and turn on the fan in the hood, which is completely outmatched. Opening some windows and fanning the smoke in their direction is, as they say, too little, too late. A moment later the smoke alarms begin beeping. I drop my face in my hands and sigh. Nothing's easy.

Chapter Ten

Aunt Beverly is lecturing me on the use (or maybe misuse is a better word) of her precious kitchen. I shouldn't be working around open flame, she says, in my condition, especially with the frequency that my flashbacks have been occurring over the past few days. That's when I tune her out. Not because I don't respect the rules of her kitchen, but I've heard them before: once when I accidentally substituted salt for sugar in a batch of cookies I'd intended to surprise her with, once when I'd given myself a pretty serious shock trying to use her electric mixer, and once, well, you get the picture. When I lost the ability to focus, I lost the ability to cook. I once burnt sushi.

When my aunt mentions the frequency of the flashbacks, though, she strikes a nerve. If somebody would have asked me just two or three days ago, I would have told them that I was just shy of being cured of these replays. I hadn't had one in weeks. Shaking? Sure. Nagging fear of airplanes? Of course. I still thought about the terrorists and how I would feel if I was living back in the big city, but the flashbacks had all but gone. Then, something, and I wish I could figure out just what that something was, triggered this onslaught. I am spending almost every waking moment of my life reliving the months that followed 9/11, in order, like they are trying to tell me a story. Almost as if they are trying to make a point. Unfortunately, I'm about as good at problem solving as I've been at cooking.

"Oh, you're not even listening to me," Aunt Beverly says. "You're hopeless."

She storms out of the room, throwing her hands up in disgust. I know she's serious, but she cracks me up sometimes and I allow myself a moment to laugh. The moment passes and I get angry again at Uncle Clint. That bastard. Cheating on Aunt Beverly. I want to believe this so bad, so I can be justified in hating him, yet the idea of some woman being attracted to him just goes against every last bit of faith I have in the female gender. It just isn't possible.

At the same time, I know what I heard.

I get up from the dining room chair, where I had been placed to be chastised, and go to the window which looks out toward the field where Uncle Clint has gone to begin mowing down the crunchy yellow corn stalks that were not harvested earlier in the year. These he'll bundle up and sell to people as decorations that will adorn their homes through Halloween and Thanksgiving, torn down and discarded just in time to be replaced by strings of lights and mechanical reindeer for Christmas.

I watch him trying to get the tractor running and am overwhelmed by an absence of sympathy for him as he struggles. Damned tractor, though. I just fixed it yesterday. He kicks the machine, then hops around in pain. This catches me by surprise and I utter a loud, belly-busting laugh. Again, the laugh is fleeting. It's hard for me to enjoy anything when I begin to think about the day ahead.

In a few minutes, I have to get ready to meet with Doctor Wallace. That thought is always enough to sober me up (though it's usually not sobering from joy to depression, but more like sobering from mild depression to clinical depression).

I look at my hands and notice the shaking has returned. It's amazing. For something that's supposed to be helping me get better, I dread therapy. I'm staring at my hand when the tractor outside backfires.

You'd think that with my paranoia being centered on such violent events, a sound so similar to gunfire would remind me of some incident that involved gunfire. Nope. It reminds me of a car backfiring.

I'm back in New York City after the reading of the will. The ride back was terrifying and almost came to an abrupt end somewhere in the suburbs. When the skyline came into view, I wanted to turn around, retreat, tuck-tail-and-run, but somehow I forced myself onward and eventually found myself here, outside the car rental office waiting for a cab. That's when it happens.

BANG!

Without a second thought, I hit the deck shaking like a scolded puppy, but I still have the presence of mind to thank God for my quick reflexes. There are probably dozens of people on the street who are not as ready for this as I am. They couldn't possibly have reacted as quickly as I did. One of them is probably lying dead in the street, a victim of his own inability to believe the terrorists would try something again.

I hug the concrete, pressing myself to it, trying to merge into it, just in case the gunfire continues. The ground is ice against my skin, but I endure, knowing that every second I can bear the cold is another second that I am prolonging my life. Within seconds, I begin to shiver, but I'm not sure if it's the cold or my nerves.

I wait until there is a good minute without shots being fired before I dare lift my head from the sidewalk. Slowly, I look up, expecting to see a dead body or maybe some hostages, but before I can focus I begin to realize that the noises of the city never ceased.

As my gaze travels upward, I see shoes, legs, belt buckles, shirt buttons, all turned in my direction: a circle of people standing around me, staring. Nobody is asking if I am okay and nobody is calling 911. They are just staring. Some aren't even fully stopping, they're just slowing down, twisting as if their eyes were attached to me by a hook and fishing line. I'm a spectacle. If they're lucky, maybe they'll get to see some blood, maybe they'll get to tell their friends how they saw a crazy man die on the street, but either way it will be a good story.

I rise up to one knee and plant my other foot on the ground, like a sprinter getting into his starting position. Maybe that's not such a bad plan to keep in mind. I may just want to run from here as fast as I can.

There's a man standing next to me wearing a bloodied apron. The sight of the blood makes me think, briefly, that I had been right about the gunshot, until I realize the man is the butcher from the shop just behind us. He stares at me, then shakes his head. Realizing there is no danger, at least not from terrorists, I rise to my feet.

"What happened?" the butcher asks. The question doesn't have the tone of concern, it's got more of an annoyed sound to it—almost as if it says, *Hey, Pal, your nut-job antics are drawing a crowd of people that aren't spending money in my store, but they're sure as hell doing a good job of blocking the entrance.*

I look around, confused, and mutter, "But, the gunshot ..."

"Dude," a young man in front of me says, "it was a car backfiring."

My cheeks grow warm as I begin to feel a similar embarrassment to the one I felt the night I ran into my co-workers at their happy hour. I brush off my clothes and try to feign a little pride. I mumble some type of apology, completely unaware of why I feel I need to apologize to anyone, before quickly making my way through the crowd to the curb. I hail a cab which can't arrive quickly enough.

When the taxi pulls to the curb, I practically leap into the back seat, but freeze before the door clicks shut. I'm staring at the back of a turban and visions of nuclear sugarplums start dancing in my head. I feel dizzy and nauseous.

"Where to?" he asks, but I don't hear that. Instead it sounds more like, "Ba Boom?"

I jump from the cab, knocking a few gawkers aside, and sprint down the sidewalk. How the hell am I supposed to get around? Trains and subways are just too easy a target for the terrorists. Bridges and tunnels, too. The cabs are being driven by *them.* Am I forced to commute to work each day in a horse-drawn carriage? Go food shopping in a Rickshaw? Maybe boogie-board to the Laundromat on a rainy day?

People are flowing by, unaware of the death traps that surround them. I wish I could wake them up. I wish I could make them see what I see, but I already know that it's useless. I glance up at the street sign to get my bearings.

8th Avenue.

I look around and try to find something that looks familiar. I'm so close to home, I know I am, yet everything seems so foreign, so alien. My heart is racing and black spots are floating in front of my eyes. I need to sit and I need to sit quickly.

I turn down the next street and see a bar on the corner. A beer is definitely what I need. As I approach, I read the sign above the window. *The Slaughtered Lamb.* No, I can't go there. The name is just too ominous. I can only imagine what would happen in there. Slaughter is not on my list of things to do today.

I spin around and spot another sign across the street. *Down the Hatch.* Okay, I can't find anything wrong there. After a moment my mind starts to conjure up what kind of terrorist connotations the name might have, but I somehow manage to force these thoughts down. I need that beer.

The sign hangs above a staircase that leads down into the basement of the building. Claustrophobia tugs at my ear as I begin to descend, but I refuse to listen. I open the steel door and move straight ahead to the bar. It's a small bar, dark and fairly quiet. College basketball plays on the televisions mounted on the wall.

"What can I get you?" the bartender asks, throwing a cardboard coaster in front of me.

"A beer. Any beer," I say.

The bartender nods and turns to the taps.

"Wait," I say.

He stops.

"Domestic."

He pours me a nice golden draft and puts it on the bar in front of me. I stare down into the brew and the bartender stares down at me.

"You okay?" he asks.

I glance up. I didn't realize he was still standing there. The television sounds so freakin' loud right now, I feel like my head will split open.

"Oh, no, no, I'm fine," I lie. I look around the room and realize nobody is paying attention to the game. "Could you turn that down just a bit?"

"The game?" He turns to the television and hits the volume. "The sound's practically off, dude. You sure you're okay?"

"Ever been at a really loud, really chaotic party?" I ask him.

He leans in to me and says, "Do you see where I work?"

"Good point. Well, let me put it this way. Picture a Friday night here. Work's letting out and people are just starting to filter in. The noise level is picking up, the pace behind the bar is quickening. You decide to take a break before the real crowd hits. You stand out back somewhere, take a smoke, and enjoy the silence. Then you come back inside and the late crowd has hit earlier than expected. It's so loud you can't hear yourself think. The room is utter chaos. You can't even keep up with popping beer bottle tops, let alone pouring drafts and mixing drinks. Ever have that night?"

He nods. "Often."

"Right now, that night is my life."

"What did you say?" he asks, but before I can move my lips to answer, I realize that the man's voice has suddenly changed. It's older now and feminine.

My mind goes cloudy for a moment, while I try to figure out just where I am and what it is I'm doing. Then the voice speaks again.

"Jim?" Aunt Beverly asks.

"Huh?" I mutter.

"Did you say something, just now?" she asks as she dusts the furniture around me.

"No," I say, shaking my head, "not just now."

CHAPTER ELEVEN

Twelve-thirty in the afternoon is the time when I get ready to go visit Dr. Wallace. I call him my therapist, but he is a full-fledged psychiatrist. Aunt Beverly insisted on it. She's not a big fan of psychology, but realizing that I did need some help, she insisted it be a psychiatrist because at least, she said, they are medical doctors. Anyone can put a piece of paper on the wall and call themselves a therapist, she insisted, and she wasn't about to let some amateur get into her nephew's head.

I pull a hand-knit sweater over my head, not caring for a moment that it makes half the hairs on my head stand on-end with static electricity. I slip my well-worn sneakers onto my feet and head out to the living room. I'm not looking forward to the next part.

Through the window, I see Uncle Clint sitting in the cab of his beat-up yellow pickup truck smoking his pipe while he waits for me. Aunt Beverly doesn't drive and she won't let me behind the wheel of a car. She didn't let me drive when I was having infrequent blackouts so there's no way in hell she would change her mind now. I'm doomed to spend the next forty-five minutes in a smoke-filled truck listening to Hank Williams, Jr. and smelling Uncle Clint. Yes, even through the pipe smoke I will be able to smell him. My stomach turns when I think about it, but there's no alternative.

I plant a kiss on Aunt Beverly's cheek and leave the house without a word. She knows I don't look forward to therapy days because I often regress after my session, at least for a few hours and sometimes as long as a day. I attribute it to bringing up all of these past, painful memories and figure that after some time my mind adjusts. Whether I'm actually better or not after that, who knows. There's no sanity meter so it's all relative. This week, in particular, I'm pretty worried. I mean, I've pretty much regressed already over the past two days, what the hell's going to happen after my session?

I get into the car and *Whiskey Bent and Hell Bound* is playing on the cassette player. Hank Williams, Jr. Never fails. I hate country music, but because of my weekly car ride with Uncle Clint, I can recite almost every song on the greatest hits tape. At least he puts the pipe out when he begins to drive.

We pull away from the house and my dread sets in. I dread the awkward silence of the car ride, I dread the therapy session, and I dread the even more awkward silence of the car ride home—that's when I know Uncle Clint is wondering just what kind of freak show went on inside the doctor's office. I listen as the ground crunches under the tires, wishing it was the only sound that I would hear along the way.

"Not havin' one of those flashbacks, are ya?" Uncle Clint asks, completely setting my universe off-kilter.

Damn! I not only *thought* it would be awkward silence all the way to the doctor's office, I *knew* it. Now, my Uncle Eloquence has decided to unleash his tongue, most likely to poison me with his lies and infidelities. Double Damn! There's no choice but to respond and I think long and hard about what to say. Finally, when I have it phrased just right, I blurt it out.

"No."

"That's good," he says.

I look at him, my brow creased. "Uh, yeah. Yeah it is."

This is going well.

"They hurt?" he asks.

Yup, that's right. He asks if they hurt. Oh God, why does he have to speak? I look out the window, wishing for a nuclear bomb or some kind of attack that will end this excruciating exchange. Is this all I needed all along? Uncle Clint tries to have a conversation with me and I suddenly embrace all my fears.

"Um, nope. No pain."

"Hmm," he grunts.

Then he actually asks something fairly intelligent. He asks it quietly, though, without much confidence. I can barely hear him over Hank.

"Why'd they start again?"

I don't answer. I stare straight ahead at the road. We're coming up on the back end of a Dodge Ram and I begin to wish Uncle Clint would just slam his foot on the accelerator, but he doesn't. Instead, a few drops of rain splatter down on the windshield as the blinker clicks and we casually pass the other car. So much for a quick and painless end.

"Something. I don't know what, but something started it." He must know that I know about his affair. He's being too friendly.

Up ahead the city looms, dark and foreboding, with a storm cloud sitting directly overhead. I try not to focus on the city itself. I try to think about the appointment and all the good it will do me. Maybe we'll be able to figure out why this is happening again. Maybe I won't panic. Maybe I won't completely and utterly freak out. Maybe the crowds won't scare me. Maybe I won't think that every vehicle is a car-bomb. Maybe …

Who am I trying to kid? My heart is already racing. A cold sweat has broken out on my brow. I want to pee. A lot. If I wasn't concentrating so hard, I might have by now.

I look at the skyline, gray and dead. This was the toughest part of therapy early on. Heading into a city. I had come out here to escape the city, but the only recommendations we got for psychiatrists were all in Colorado Springs. The buildings were definitely not the same as New York, not as high, but that didn't matter. It was a city. In fact there were only two reasons I was able to make it: NORAD and the United States Air Force Academy. I could see the glowing ring of NORAD in the mountainside as we entered the city and that was a tremendous comfort. The defenses of North America were headquartered there. That, accompanied by the Air Force Academy, gave me a fairly decent amount of confidence that any plane going off-course would be shot down before it could do any damage.

Maybe that was true. Maybe it wasn't. Thank God I never found out. It never eradicated my fear, but it was enough to get me through.

Now, heading into the city once again, I feel that paralyzing fear tempered by the small amount of security that I've come to know. I watch the skyline grow nearer and larger. One minute it is Colorado Springs and the next it morphs into a skyline much more familiar to me. It is probably *the* most recognizable skyline in the world; it is the skyline that was drastically changed on that September day back in 2001. Colorado Springs has become New York City.

I notice right away that, thankfully, I am not getting any closer. There's only a moment to glance around and absorb the fact that Uncle Clint and his pick-up truck have vanished before the memories of them follow. A cold wind blows against my face. It seems I've been sitting out here for quite a while because my cheeks are numb from the cold.

After a few beers at *Down the Hatch*, the bartender was kind enough to call me a cab (which luckily had an American driver) that could take me out of the city to a hotel in Fort Lee, NJ. It's not far from the city, but it *is* outside the city.

I'm on the balcony of my rented room watching cars make their way across the George Washington Bridge. They blend into a string of white lights and a string of red lights stretching from one bank of the Hudson River to the other. Upper deck, lower deck. They move with what seems to be utter lack of fear and hesitation. At least that's how it appears to me.

Across the river, the city mocks me. "Can't handle me?" it screeches, in a shrill, inhuman voice. "Can't take what I've got to give?"

I turn away, but the break in eye contact doesn't silence the city. It knows what I'm thinking, what I want. "Go ahead," it whispers now, "make the call. Embarrass yourself further."

I flip open my cell phone in defiance. The numbers on the keypad illuminate my face with their electric blue glow. I look at the skyline and hold my open phone out to it, but I haven't dialed and that damned city knows it.

With my hands trembling like a frightened baby bunny, I scroll through my contact list until Andrew's name is highlighted. My finger hovers over the Send button, but I can't press down.

"AAAAHHHHHHHHHH," I scream out into the frigid night air. I wind up as if I'm going to throw my phone all the way across the river, but I can't bring myself to do it. Rather than let the phone go when I swing my arm, I clench my fist tight around it all the way into my follow-through.

"Damn!"

I kick the balcony chair and walk back into the room, muttering vulgarities under my breath. Stopping to stare at the phone in my hand, I realize I've got to do this. If I don't, it will be over. Andrew is my anchor and if I don't speak to him right now, I may float away, never to return.

I flip the phone back open, hesitate, then turn to draw the drapes closed. That's better. Now the damned city can no longer taunt me. With concentration and determination that makes my temples throb, I punch each individual key—each familiar number, one after the other. Then I wait.

Ring one.

Ring two.

I tense up when I realize she probably won't answer. She screens my calls much more often now.

The third ring comes and I'm ready to hang up, but it's interrupted.

"Hello?"

It's a small voice. A little high-pitched, but not a woman's voice. It's a little boy's voice.

"Andrew?" I ask, my heart pounding rapidly in my chest. "Is that you?"

"Daddy?"

A tear builds on my eyelid, but I refuse to let myself cry. If I do, I'll lose it. I need to be strong.

"Drew? It's so good to hear your voice."

"I miss you, Daddy," he whispers. That's when I realize that something's not right.

"Drew, where's Mommy?"

"In the shower. Daddy, why won't Mommy let me talk to you anymore?"

I try to speak, but the words get lodged in my throat. I take a deep breath.

"What do you mean, Drew? Of course you can talk to me."

"Mommy says that I'm not gonna talk to you anymore. She says we're going away."

My previously fluttering heart comes to a complete halt. Away? Where could they possibly be going? How could she even think that I wouldn't be talking to my son anymore?

"That's not going to happen. Daddy won't let that happen."

"I don't want to go away, Daddy. I want to see you. I miss you."

He's crying now and my dormant heart takes a nose-dive right into the pit of my gut. I want to throw-up. How could she fill this poor little boy's head with such lies? How could she make him worry over nothing?

"Don't cry, Drew. Daddy will come get you."

There's a commotion on the other end, some indiscernible voices, then my wife's voice comes on the line. "Hello?"

"Hello, Rebecca," I say, managing to keep my own voice calm, my temper in check.

"Oh geez," she sighs. "Hello, Jim. He's not supposed to answer the phone."

"Is that to keep him from telling me that you're going away? What the hell was that all about Rebecca?"

More sighing.

"Were you just going to up and leave without telling me? Where do you think ..."

"Enough," she snaps. Then in a whisper, "Enough."

I remain silent, waiting for the explanation, if there could possibly be one. My muscles are tense, my heart is racing, and I'm gripping my cell phone so tight my knuckles are white.

"You weren't supposed to find out this way."

"How the hell was I supposed to find out? When I called and somebody new had your number? When I stopped by to visit because I hadn't been able to get in touch with you for so long, only to find your apartment empty? Would that have been better for you, Rebecca? Less painful for you? More convenient?"

She doesn't say anything for a while—a very long while. "Jim, it would have been easier for Andrew. I'm going now. *We're* going. Good-bye."

"Wait! Rebecca, you can't ..."

The click at the other end cuts me short. I stare down at the silent phone in my hand and I can almost see the searing blood coursing through my veins. Exploding with rage, I spin around and wing the phone against the wall where it collides with a framed print. The glass of the frame shatters into a million tiny pieces and crashes to the floor.

The neighbor thumps on the wall, but I barely hear as I sink to the bed and cover my face with my hands. In my mind, I can still hear Andrew's voice. I can hear him tell me that he misses me. I want so badly to reach out and hold him, but I know I can't. In fact, I'll probably never hold him again.

Feeling hollow, I let out a loud sob.

"Whazzat?" Uncle Clint grunts.

I snap my head up at the sound of his voice. Uncle Clint, the truck, Hank Williams, Jr. and Colorado Springs are all back. The difference is, we're in Colorado Springs, not outside of it.

"Nothing. It was nothing."

CHAPTER TWELVE

Dr. Wallace's office is dark—darker than I ever thought a psychiatrist's office would be. These places are supposed to be comforting and inviting or at least that's what I always imagined. This office is anything but that. The walls are lit by sconces that project a small half-moon of light upward. These patches are the only area in the room where you can see the wall color. Some interior decorator mistook *softly lit* for *barely lit* and, frankly, it creeps me out.

The furniture is not only minimalist, it's sparse. A desk, a bookcase, a chair, and a couch are all that occupy the small space. There are too many books for the bookcase and they've spilled over onto all available surfaces in the office. The desk is cluttered with folders and the walls are adorned with children's artwork. At least I think they were created by children. Some of the subject matter is so bizarre I pray it couldn't have come from the mind of a child.

I sit on the couch, as usual, while Dr. Wallace uses the men's room. I never actually lie down like you see in the movies. Maybe I'm just rebellious. Who knows?

After a few moments, Dr. Wallace returns to the office. I suspect, sometimes, that he doesn't really need to go to the men's room, but he uses the time as his little power-grab: the *remember, we're here on my time* ruse. He enters the room without a word, as if he's preoccupied with his all-important thoughts. He sits at his desk without acknowledging me, shuffles through some papers and stuffs a copy of the DSM-IV onto a shelf. It's a big, thick book with a lot of psychological disorders in it. I'm sure they've got a whole chapter dedicated to me.

"Good book, huh?" I say, attempting a bit of small talk.

Dr. Wallace lifts his head and looks at me as if he had no idea I was in the room with him. He glances at his watch, making sure our conversation is no longer free. I guess we're either on my dime or close enough to it, because he decides to answer.

"It's got an incredible amount of information, Jim, but already it's becoming outdated. Revision five is in the works, but it will be another few years before we get our hands on it."

That was a whole hell of a lot more information than I wanted, or cared about, but I nod politely anyway. He comes over to the chair and sits, cross-legged. I once tried to sit that way after spending an hour here. It wasn't comfortable, actually it was borderline painful, but he does it like he enjoys it. Oh well, to each his own.

He takes his yellow legal pad from a sleeve on the side of the chair and pulls a pen from his pocket. He clicks the pen and jots something on the paper. It's most likely the date and time, or something like that, but I like to think he's writing something along the lines of, "2:30 pm, time for nutball Jim again."

"How have you been, Jim?" he asks. "Last time we spoke you seemed to be doing very well with your shaking and flashbacks."

"Yeah, about that," I say, with a sarcastic, yet obviously uncomfortable chuckle.

"Did something happen?"

"Yes. Well, no, not really. Like, I didn't *do* anything. Nothing *physically* happened. The flashbacks, though, they came back. With a vengeance. I've been having them every few hours over the past two days. Practically one right after the other."

"Triggers?"

"I've recognized each one, just like you explained. Problem is, I can't really avoid them or face them head-on. They're all so trivial, so banal."

"Why don't you tell me some of them?"

"Let's see, there was footsteps, there was knots in some wood, there was a shower, some powdered sugar, oh, forks and knives clinking on plates, that one was fantastic. What else, the city skyline—one of the more obvious ones, y'know? Oh, right, the slamming of a door. So what do you think? Should I go slam a few doors and desensitize myself to the whole thing?"

"There's no need for sarcasm, Jim. Tell me what they were about, if you can remember."

Remember? How could I forget? It gets pretty easy to remember something after you've relived it for the second, third, or fourth time. As many times as I've tried to explain this to Dr. Wallace, he still insists that the flashbacks are dreamlike. He still thinks that I can direct the outcome of the *storylines* with some conscious effort. He doesn't grasp that I'm re-experiencing my past. I think he wants them to be dreams so that he could find a nice, snug Freudian psychoanalytical theory to slip around them, tie them up with a nice little bow and say, *hey, here's your diagnosis.* Unfortunately, I'm not that easy.

I spend the time, however, explaining each and every flashback to him in detail. The stories are nothing he hasn't heard already. Whether I've flashed back to these particular times in my life before is irrelevant. The fact is, when I started my sessions I had to give him my whole back-story. There should be no part of my past that is unfamiliar to him.

"Jim," he says, then he pauses and takes his glasses off. He rubs the bridge of his nose before putting the glasses back on. "Were you able to identify *the* trigger? Not the ones that sparked the individual flash-backs, but the one that started the whole progression of them."

I think for a minute, but can't come up with anything. I try, damn do I try, but no matter what, I can't come up with something that might have set this off.

"No, not that I know of. It just started. One second I'm standing on the porch with Aunt Beverly, then she leaves and I'm years in the past. That was the first of many over the past two days."

"Hmm, so you're aunt left you there on the porch? How did that make you feel?"

"C'mon, doc. It's not like she's never left me alone before. I can deal with that. I mean, I remember thinking that she was the only family I had left, but she walked away. That's not a big deal."

"Maybe not consciously, Jim, but maybe symbolically it is."

"What are you talking about?" I ask. He always makes my head spin.

"You said yourself that you feel she is the only family that you have left, correct?"

"As much as I'd like to say that's not true, realistically, I'd have to say that it is."

"Because Rebecca and Andrew are gone?"

Using their names in that phrase still eats at me. I hate him for bringing it up, but I trust he knows what he's doing.

"Yeah, because of that."

He nods and scribbles something on his pad.

"Did this particular thought of your aunt being the only family you have left occupy your mind significantly?"

I start to tell him no, but then I hesitate. It was only a brief thought, but it had hurt. Now that I think about it, it had hurt really bad.

"I guess," I say, not willing to commit to his theory yet.

More scribbling, some jotting, and he pauses. "Tell me more about what you were thinking that morning on the porch."

I hear him make this suggestion, but I'm tuning him out. To me, Dr. Wallace suddenly feels a thousand miles away. I can hear him, barely, and I do my best to focus on his voice, but he keeps slipping. In the distance, I hear my name called repeatedly. "Jim? Jim are you there? Jim?"

The voice grows louder, but it's no longer Dr. Wallace's voice. In fact, all memories of Dr. Wallace quickly fade like a dream soon after waking. The voice is that of my boss.

"Jim, are you still there?"

I look at the phone in my hand and cautiously put it back to my ear.

"Um, yeah," I stammer. "Sorry, what was the question?"

"Don't play games with me, Jim. Where the hell have you been? You've been gone for almost a week and this is the first I hear from you. Give me one good reason why I shouldn't fire you right now."

God, I hate this guy. I wanted to go back to work, I really did, but it turns out our offices have returned to a new suite in New York and I can't go back into the city. I tried. That night after the phone call with Andrew and Rebecca, I tried. I gathered up all the courage I could muster, gritted my teeth and hopped in a taxi. I even fought the panic when it turned out to be an Arab taxi cab driver. My son was all that mattered. We had gotten maybe three or four blocks from my hotel when I started to realize I would soon be at the point where turning around was no longer an option. If I got onto the George Washington Bridge, I would have no choice but to go into Manhattan. Frantically, I pleaded for the cab driver to turn around and silently prayed that he wasn't a terrorist hell-bent on transporting my heathen-American ass into the city to add to the inevitable death toll.

Luckily for me, he wasn't and I was returned safely to my hotel. I stood out front for a while, the bitter cold wind biting at my face and hands and tearing its way through the thin layer of clothes I had on. I hadn't even stopped to grab my jacket on the way out. How could I get back there? How could I stop my wife from taking my son away from me?

In the end, I hadn't been able to find a way. No means of transportation would be different. Train, ferry, bus, and taxi. No matter which I took, once I was on my way, I was a prisoner. Hell, even if I rented a car and drove myself, the tunnels and bridges made it impossible to even think about retreating. The next week was spent living in a hotel room eating room service which I make the waiters leave outside the door. I'm not even sure I've showered in that time and, with the exception of maybe a couple of hours, the television hasn't been on. I won't allow them to deliver a newspaper to me, either. I need to be alone, without the influences of the outside world.

"I'm having a hard time, here, Tom."

It's meant to stall so that I can come up with the one thousand and one good reasons why he shouldn't fire me. I know they exist, but for some strange reason I just can't come up with them at the moment. Think!

"As are we, Jim, being a man short."

"Tom, it's just that my cell phone wasn't working. Um, I dropped it and, well, I ..."

I stop. I really don't have anything. I've got no reason, no excuse, nothing. I let out a deep sigh.

"I've got no reason, Tom. None whatsoever."

I hear his tension ease on the other side of the phone. I don't know how, I just hear it. I've given him his out. I've just basically given him permission to cut loose the dead weight that's been dragging him down for six months, the parasite who's been collecting checks from him without actually doing anything. Even when I've been at the office my production has been non-existent. I've just handed my executioner the ax.

"Well then, Jim, I think we have nothing more to say. Your position will be terminated immediately. Your checks will be mailed unless you have direct deposit, in which case they will continue to be deposited into your account for the remainder of what we owe you. Frankly, Jim, whatever it is, I think it's too much. Are there any questions?"

There should be, but there aren't. I just wait.

"Fine. Good-bye."

And with that, the call ends. I place the phone back into the cradle and think about who I need to call to explain that I've lost my job, but nobody comes to mind. The only one who would have cared would have been the hotel manager when I stopped being able to pay the bill, but at least I have my inheritance to help me through that. I'll be back on my feet in no time, really. I'll get right out there tomorrow and start looking for a job. Yup, that's what I'll do.

I lie back on the bed and stare at the ceiling, fantasizing about all the wonderful jobs that will be available to me in New Jersey. I study the stucco patterns in the ceiling, but suddenly the bright lights of my hotel room are gone. I don't know if the room has gone dark or if something has happened to my vision, but I soon realize I'm no longer in New Jersey. I'm back in Colorado Springs at Dr. Wallace's office and, for the first time ever, I am actually lying down on his couch.

Christ. I can't even get through a single session with my psychiatrist without blacking out. I turn my head to see Dr. Wallace sitting there watching me. He raises an eyebrow in my direction and I sigh.

"Yup," I say to his unspoken question, "that was another one."

"At least now I've gotten to experience one first hand," he says.

"You should try it from my point of view."

Chapter Thirteen

My session ends without further incident. Dr. Wallace poked and prodded my brain for a while, but I'm pretty sure he was unsuccessful at whatever it was he was trying to do. He mumbled some words here and there that sounded like they might have been diagnoses, but he told me to come back next week, so I guess I'm not better yet. One of these weeks I expect him to cure me or eventually I'm going to want my money back.

When I return to the truck, it's empty. I'm not surprised. With each trip into the city, Uncle Clint's visits to the nearby bar have become longer and longer. I can't imagine he's doing anything in there but sitting alone in a dark corner, drinking straight whiskey, and leering at all the younger women, which most likely would be every woman in the place.

I wait by the pickup for a few minutes, but the truth is I'm not feeling so hot. My mind feels totally violated, as if Dr. Wallace had just reached in, mashed it around a bit, and exposed it for all the world to see. All I want to do is get the hell home. I lean against the pickup, check my watch, stare at the bar, look back at my watch, lean some more. I'm leaning now with a ferocious intensity. Hell, nobody could possibly match the angry impatience with which I lean against this stupid truck. I figure if I just lean a little harder, Uncle Clint will show up.

After a few minutes of this inactivity, I figure I'm actually going to have to do something in order to get his butt out here. I push myself off the car and walk down the street to the bar, open the front door and head in. It is so bright outside that my eyes take a long time to adjust to the small amount of light inside.

I stumble around, my arms outstretched like a man trying to find his way to the bathroom in the middle of the night after waking up in a strange place. After a few moments, my sight adjusts and I see Uncle Clint sitting at a corner table, watching me. He's not offering help by waving or calling my name and it's not as though he doesn't see me. Apparently, he's just finding some warped entertainment in watching me trip around the room. As I approach his table, I realize he wasn't the only one enjoying a chuckle at my expense. Most of the patrons are throwing a joke or a comment my way. Great, a whole bar full of Uncle Clints. Have I reached Hell?

Humbly, I smile, bite my lip and join my uncle at his table. He still doesn't say a word to me. He just watches me with the slightest of smiles on his face.

"Maybe we should get going," I offer.

"Nah," he replies, "order yerself a drink. I just got mine."

"I'm not so sure alcohol is such a good idea. For me, at least."

"Ahhh," he grunts. He signals the bartender, points at his whiskey, then at me.

"I don't even drink whiskey," I whisper at him. I'm starting to get a little annoyed now. "Besides, you have to drive."

"I'll be fine," he growls. "Besides, whiskey'll put some hair on your chest. Make ya a man."

Great, just what I need: lessons from a fat, slovenly unfaithful hick on how to be a man. If I wanted to be the evil twin of Barney the drunk from *The Simpsons*, I'd listen. The whiskey is slammed down in front of me. Some of it spills onto the table which is already giving off enough flammable vapors that a passerby smoking a cigarette would end up engulfing us in flames.

Uncle Clint waits silently, until the pure discomfort of the situation forces me to take a drink. I slam the glass back, hoping to swallow every last bit before my taste buds know what's going on. I wince and realize what a terrible plan that was. After I'm done gagging, my uncle orders me another.

"At least get me a glass of water," I beg. He nods and reluctantly asks the waitress to bring some for me.

"So what'd the doc say?" he asks.

Great.

"Something about separation anxiety," I say, matter-of-factly. I'm hoping he doesn't know what that means and is too proud to make himself feel stupid by asking.

"What's that mean?" he asks. I should have known. This man has no fear of making himself look stupid.

I sigh. This *is* Hell. You think there would have been some kind of warning. Some sign at the gate saying, "You are about to enter Hell. Caution: Hot flames and annoying, ignorant people. Proceed at your own risk."

"It means I have a fear of losing the people closest to me," I offer, hoping this will end the conversation.

"Like Rebecca and Andrew. Your mother," he says, obviously impressed with his psychoanalytical abilities. His chest seems a little puffed out, but that could just be fat.

"No," I say, dragging it out to make him understand just how wrong he is. "They're already gone."

"Hmph," he grunts, nodding. "Who else ya got?"

Wow, he really knows how to make a guy feel good. Luckily he's still making himself look stupid, otherwise I'd be angry by now.

"Aunt Beverly," I respond, intentionally leaving his name off the very brief list. I hope he notices.

"Where's she goin'?"

He didn't notice. That, or he didn't care.

Hank Williams, Jr. starts to play on the jukebox. Uncle Clint's eyes light up and I smack my face into the table, coating it with a nice film of flammable liquor. I look around, hoping somebody will walk by with a cigarette, a lighter, a blowtorch, anything.

I think about that image and it brings back another that's haunted me since early 2002. It's the image of a woman being set on fire in her car. Ever since I read the story that day in my hotel room, I've had the occasional nightmare in which I'm the one in the car. I remember how nauseous I felt when I read the article. I was almost as sick to my stomach as the whiskey is making me feel now.

Did I say whiskey? Beer. I'm drinking beer. I'm sitting in my hotel room in Ft. Lee, New Jersey, drinking beer. As the bar in Colorado Springs quickly fades from my mind, I have enough time to curse myself for dwelling on a memory for too long. Then Colorado Springs is gone. Ft. Lee, New Jersey is reality and for some reason I have the strangest desire to thank God that Hank Williams, Jr. is not playing.

I stare at the newspaper sitting on the table in front of me. The hotel has been good about complying with my request to not deliver it to my room, but that doesn't mean they're going to remove the pile from the lobby. I passed by there this morning when I was taking advantage of the free continental breakfast and I made the mistake of glancing at the headlines.

One, in particular, caught my eye and I snatched a copy, hiding it beneath my arm as if I was committing a crime. I ran up to my room and shut the door, then peeked out through the peephole to make sure nobody had followed me. Not once did I think about how stupid that idea might be. Now, here I sit, maybe a half-hour later, the newspaper still folded neatly. The headline is just above the fold, so I haven't yet ventured to read anymore.

"Coroner Set to Testify in Terrorist Trial Survives Attempt on Life"

It glares at me. I want to read it. I need to read it. I haven't read a newspaper in a month. I tense my jaw and place my hands on it. I can almost feel the newsprint sticking to my fingers. I pick it up, studying it, testing its weight in my hands. It's almost a whole new experience for me. I slip my finger into the crease and let go of the bottom half of the newspaper, displaying the front page in its beautiful, unadulterated glory. My eyes scan from headline to headline, absorbing each word, savoring each picture.

Then they stop. It's the story about the coroner. My heart picks up the pace a bit and my hands tremble. I place the newspaper on the table before I begin reading in order to prevent myself from getting seasick.

The article tells of a coroner who performed autopsies on some of the people involved in the 9/11 attacks. Apparently he was attacked, bound with barbed wire, and wired with a bomb. Somehow the lucky son-of-a-bitch survived the whole thing.

I stop reading and listen carefully. I could have sworn there was a noise outside my room. Was there a terrorist in the building? Forget that they would have no reason to be watching me. Forget that millions of people around the country are reading the same article that I am now reading. Forget that there is an ice machine across the hall that rumbles every few minutes. This noise was a terrorist. That is the only explanation as far as I am concerned.

I get up from the table and look through the peep-hole again. The hallway appears empty, but that's not good enough. I secure the latch on the door, the one that lets you open it far enough to see out, but prevents the door from being kicked in. Still, the hallway is empty, but I hold my breath and listen. Nothing. I finally convince myself that it was just my imagination, so I click the door shut and leave the security latch in place before going back to the newspaper.

I continue to read the story, tearing the paper open to page two where it continues, but freeze when another headline catches my eye.

"Death of Alleged Terrorist Accomplice Ruled Homicide."

Something about that article grabs me, pulls me in. Soon I'm fully aware of the back-story of Katherine Smith, accused of helping five

Islamic terrorists get their driver's licenses. The day before she was scheduled to appear in court, her car veers off the road and crashes into a telephone pole after a fire broke out inside. They found a suicide note, but the investigation showed that she had been doused in gasoline. They had finally ruled it a homicide.

I put the paper down on the table, subconsciously rubbing my fingers together to try to clean the newsprint off them. I can't stop thinking about Katherine Smith and what she must have been going through. Maybe she helped them out. Maybe she didn't. If she did, maybe it was intentional, maybe it wasn't. Regardless of how it happened or why, that woman was killed by these monsters in a way that can, at best, be described as brutal. It just reinforces how ruthless they are. It makes me even angrier now that people refuse to see the truth. Had that been a gunshot last month instead of a car backfiring, I would have been the one to live because everyone else is ignorant or stubborn or a combination of the two. If a bullet tore through their heart or a bomb shred them to pieces, the last thing any of them would think would be, *No, this isn't happening. I'm safe here.*

They walk the city streets like the World Trade Center never crumbled to the ground. They work in skyscrapers like they never saw the footage of the planes crashing into the towers. They go to airports, bus and train stations, cross bridges and tunnels, attend sporting events and concerts, shop at their malls, gamble at their casinos, all without a second thought that maybe this is when the next strike will take place. Maybe this is where life as they know it will end.

Stupid, ignorant sheep. Every last one of them. When the time comes, I and maybe even I alone, will survive. I read the article again, filling in my own details where needed. It was a horrendous crime. It was the last way I'd choose to go out. Suddenly, the barbed wire and bomb that the coroner suffered seem like a merciful way out.

This is lunacy. They really are everywhere. Somewhere in the back of my mind I've been clinging to the remote hope that maybe everybody else is right and I'm just crazy. But this—this proves me right.

The terrorists are the cab drivers and the co-workers and the guy next to you on the elevator or subway. They are the guy pumping your gas or serving your food. Hell, they're probably even the actors and actresses on Broadway, the brokers on Wall Street and the advertising executives on Madison Avenue.

Even more frightening is the fact that even that point of view is short-sighted. These terrorists are the farmers and the truck drivers. They live in rural America and in the suburbs, not just in the city. They live in houses, apartments … hotels.

I stand up from the chair so quickly it falls to the floor. I go to the curtains and peek outside, pulling them just far enough apart to look through. No suspicious activity in the parking lot, thank God. That doesn't mean they haven't already planted bombs or taken up their sniper positions on adjacent rooftops. I blink quickly as a bead of sweat that's been making its way down my forehead drips onto my eyelashes.

I've got to stop this. I've got to get a grip. I need to talk to somebody.

Picking up the phone, I begin dialing Rebecca's number, but it only takes a moment to remember that it's no longer hers. I hang up before the ring is interrupted by the heartbreaking pre-recorded message that reminds me that the number I am dialing is no longer in service. Hand shaking, I stare at the phone trying to figure out who else I have left. My mother is gone. My wife and son are gone. Even my best friend is gone, that son-of-a-bitch. Some friend.

Panic begins to grip me. I have nobody to call. I have nobody in which to confide. Even if I did, who would take me seriously? Nobody understands this all like I do.

Not knowing why, I press the phone to my ear and I'm surprised to find out it's ringing. I must have dialed a number. I wait anxiously and curiously for a voice to answer.

"Hello?" the sweet, soft voice says.

I nearly break down in tears as a flood of relief courses through me. I slump into the chair as I try to find the right words.

"Hello, who is this?" the voice says again.

"Aunt Beverly? It's me. It's Jim."

"Oh, hello, dear. How are you?"

"Not good," I manage, my voice cracking.

"What's the matter, Jimmy? Are you okay? You can talk to me."

"I know, Aunt Beverly. I know that."

I try to choke back the tears, but I'm unsuccessful.

"I don't know what I'd do if I lost you," I cry.

"Now hush," she says. "Where is it you think I'm going?"

I can't answer. I'm crying too hard.

"Jimmy, I'm worried about you."

"Thank you." It's a strange response, but it feels so appropriate. I grip the phone tighter as if this would transmit a hug through the lines.

"You need to pick yourself up," she says, but, while I agree with her, there is something off about her voice. It's suddenly deeper and a little slurred.

"Excuse me?"

"You heard me," a distinctly male and not-so-distinctly drunk, voice says. "Pick yerself up, you're makin' a spectacle of yerself."

My eyes attempt to focus, but the room I'm in is much too dark for that. The sounds and smells of the place, though, remind me that it's a bar. It's a bar in Colorado Springs and I'm here with Uncle Clint, not in my hotel room in Fort Lee, New Jersey talking to Aunt Beverly on the telephone.

I notice that my head is down on the table so I peel my face free of the unknown substance it's been resting in. When I can finally see my uncle, I look at him with the sternest gaze that I can muster.

"Can we please get out of here now?"

CHAPTER FOURTEEN

On the ride home, there is less interaction than you'd find in a leper colony full of deaf-mutes. It's forty-five minutes of watching the white lines of the road pass by, my eyes growing heavier with each passing stripe. It's a good thing I'm not driving because I'm suffering serious bouts of highway hypnosis.

We finally pull into the long driveway of Aunt Beverly's farmhouse to find a strange man standing on the porch hailing us. Uncle Clint glances at me and I shrug. I don't know the man, but I know who he might be. He might be a certain private detective that's been asking around about me. I sit on my hands so that Uncle Clint can't see how badly they're shaking.

My uncle pulls the truck to the side of the barn and kills the ignition, mercifully silencing Hank Williams, Jr. He looks at me again and I must be visibly upset because he tells me to stay in the car.

"What are you going to do?" I stammer.

"Just sit tight."

He gets out of the truck, but instead of heading to the house, he ducks into the barn. When he emerges again, he is carrying the shotgun he was instructed to keep hidden from me. He crosses the yard, stopping about halfway across and rests the gun on his shoulder.

"Can I help you?" he asks.

The visitor looks at the gun and then over at me.

"Sir, I asked you a question," Uncle Clint says.

"I'm sorry. Is that gun really necessary?"

"A man has a right to defend his home and as of right now, I ain't got a reason to believe you're not an intruder. Fancy clothes or not."

Khakis and a button-down shirt might not be what I consider to be fancy, but who am I to criticize my uncle's methods. As the showdown continues, Aunt Beverly steps out onto the porch.

"Clint?" she asks.

"Get back in the house, Beverly. I don't want you around here if I need to use this."

Without argument, my aunt hurries back inside.

"Sir, I assure you that won't be necessary," the man says, his voice a bit shaky, but gaining confidence. "I just need a few words with your nephew, Jim."

"You seem to know a lot about us, but we don't know a thing about you, mister."

"Listen …" the man begins, but he is cut short by the clicking sound of two hammers being cocked and the sight of a double barrel pointed at his face.

"I don't think I like your tone, mister. So you got less time than it takes fer a jackrabbit to git it done to tell me why you're here, otherwise I'll blow a hole through you where you stand."

The man swallows hard and takes a deep breath. I give him credit; he maintains composure fairly well for a man staring down the barrel of a shotgun.

"Your nephew knew some people back in New Jersey. I've been sent by one of them to find him. It is very important I speak with him."

This cannot be good. I want to slink under the dashboard and pretend like this isn't happening, but I can't let my uncle shoot a man down because of me. I run my hands back through my hair, clasp my fingers behind my head and squeeze my elbows together like I'm trying to squeeze courage in through my ears. Finally, I force my hand to grasp the door handle and pull. I'm out of the truck and behind Uncle Clint before I can think to stop myself, which is good because Uncle Clint's finger seems to be just one nervous twitch away from depressing the trigger.

"Who sent you?" I ask. Uncle Clint keeps the gun leveled at the stranger.

"For now, my client's name is just Matthew."

"Well, I've known a few Matthews in my life."

"But that's the only way you would have known him. Well, that and one other way."

I don't sense any immediate danger from this man, so I tell my uncle it's okay to lower the gun. He does, but he doesn't leave my side.

"What's the other way?"

"His online handle: Die4USA."

Suddenly my legs can't support me. My knees give and I grab my uncle's shoulders to steady myself. I want to say that I've never heard that name before, but I'm sure my reaction has already betrayed that notion.

"I know that name must bring up some bad memories, but he wants to talk to you. Actually, he *needs* to talk to you. He's already spoken to everybody else."

"How did you find me?"

"It wasn't easy. You guys never exchanged any personal information and your online ID's were all anonymous. Lucky for me, one of the guys in your little group worked at DMV and had copied down the license plates. Even then it wasn't easy to track you since you rode that day in somebody else's truck."

"So then how did you do it?" I ask, standing on my own now, but not wanting to hear the answer.

He hesitates, apparently knowing I do not want to hear the answer.

"I had to visit Julius."

The name strikes me like an outside linebacker coming in hard on the blind-side. My fists clench along with my jaw. I tremble a little, but I'm not sure if it's fear or outright fury.

"I had to convince him I was there to find the rest of you to, y'know, bring you all to justice," he continues.

"Why *were* you there? What do you want from me?" I look over at Uncle Clint's shotgun and consider how easy it would be to pick it up, turn it on myself, pull the trigger. As always, though, I dismiss the idea and try to steel my resolve.

"I'd rather my client explain that to you personally."

Thoughts of Julius and that day back in New Jersey are swimming around my head now, bogging it down. I try to speak but I'm afraid vomit will escape my mouth instead. I clamp my mouth shut, swallow hard and take a deep breath.

"I need to go inside," I manage to say through my teeth. The stranger tries to interrupt me, but I put up my hand in warning. There's nothing more I can discuss right now.

"I have your card," I tell him. "If you leave now, I'll consider calling you when I can talk about this. If you don't, I don't know what will happen." I throw a glance at the shotgun and the man nods. Without another word he walks off to his car.

Aunt Beverly, seeing that the danger appears to be over, comes back outside. I force a smile at her so she'll know right away that things are okay.

"Julius?" Uncle Clint whispers.

I nod. I once told my uncle about Julius, and to my knowledge he's never told another soul—not even Aunt Beverly.

He looks at me inquisitively, but lets it drop. He nods in understanding and I nod in return.

"Thank you," I whisper.

He shrugs. "There was a stranger on my property. Coulda been here to rape the women and steal the sheep, or the other way around." He winks at me and lets out a small laugh before walking toward the house. I think it's the first time I've ever heard him make a joke and it was even a little funny.

We climb the porch steps and Aunt Beverly receives me with a big hug. She leans back and crushes my face between the palms of her hands.

"Are you okay, dear?" she asks. I nod to let her know I'm fine.

"What was that about?" she asks Uncle Clint.

"Nothin' Bev. Let it go," he replies as he walks past her.

"Clinton Simms, have you been drinking whiskey?"

He grunts and continues into the house. She follows, calling after him. "How many times have I told you not to drink and drive. I ought to ..." Her voice fades away as the two of them disappear further inside and I'm left standing alone on the porch.

I go to the rail and look out into the field. My hand is still trembling and I realize that this is the exact spot in which I was standing yesterday when the whole onslaught of flashbacks started. What was it? What the hell started it all? And now this private detective? Nothing could be good about one of those guys trying to contact me.

As I reel through the possibilities in my head, I look around at everything, trying to find something that could have triggered my flashbacks, but nothing stands out and nothing causes another one to occur. I look out at the corn, I study the wooden rail, I focus on everything I was concentrating on at the time that this began yesterday morning, but nothing seems like it could have caused this. Could Dr. Wallace have been right? Could I be suffering this attack simply because I feel that Aunt Beverly might desert me? Jesus, is that how fragile my mind is these days?

"Jim, come on in. Dinner's ready," Aunt Beverly calls.

When she says this I take notice of the growing (and growling) void that is my stomach. I go inside to the dining room and pull my seat from the table.

"Wash your hands," my aunt calls from the other room, catching me just a moment before my butt hits the chair.

I huff, then stand back up and head off to the washroom, but not before noticing Uncle Clint's place conspicuously missing from the table.

"Uncle Clint isn't joining us?" I ask as I walk down the hallway.

"No. That man needs a nap. And don't think I didn't smell that whiskey on you either, young man. I don't want to see you picking up on your uncle's bad habits."

That's certainly not something she needs to worry about. I go into the washroom and wash my hands at the ornate ceramic pedestal sink. As usual, I hesitate before drying them on the hand-towel which looks as if it's meant for decoration, not for actual use.

Clean, I go back toward the dining room, but stop short when I hear whispers coming from the bedroom. I tiptoe along the runner, hoping the floorboards won't creak, and stop outside Aunt Beverly's room where Uncle Clint's muffled voice is droning on and on. I place my ear to the door and try to make out some of what he's saying, but not only is he behind a door, he's also speaking quietly. What a sneaky bastard. My recent gratitude quickly disappears. Maybe he did stand up for me out there, but here he is, just minutes later, off to his secret lover while Aunt Beverly is slaving away in the kitchen over a meal he isn't even going to eat.

His voice is getting a little louder now, so I press my ear harder against the door, but suddenly the talking stops and the door opens. I fall into the room, a less-than-pleasant impact with Uncle Clint's barrel-chest the only thing that keeps me from smacking the footboard of his bed head-first. Stupid, stupid, stupid.

"Hi," I manage as I right myself.

"Boy, what the hell are you doing?"

"Um, just seeing if you were coming to dinner," I stammer. "Aunt Beverly said you were sleeping, but then I heard you talking."

His demeanor suddenly changes from anger to concern. Something is definitely going on. He looks me over and asks, "What did you hear?"

I stare at Uncle Clint without answering. It's not because I can't come up with a good excuse, a lie of some kind, it's because he looks different. Thinner, younger. His hair has become dark and greasy. I feel like I just watched it grow until it hung limply over his eyes. He's slouched over and he smells of beer and onions. The farmhouse has transformed, too, into a small hotel room with colorful prints on the walls, a television, a couple of beds and a dresser. There's not much else.

It's December 2002, and I've switched rooms almost every week since March. I figure if I'm unpredictable it will make it more difficult for them to keep track of me, to tap my phones, to sneak-attack me when I leave my room. I'm trying to stay one step ahead of them, regardless of the fact that I have never even seen one of *them*.

The man next to me? That's Julius. We met online on a message board for people who really understand what's going on. Don't get me wrong, I didn't trust him right away. I questioned him relentlessly when he suggested that we should get together. He told me that he felt I was really the only one who genuinely knew what I was talking about. The rest of the people posting on the board? Posers. Their theories were ridiculous. Their ideas were a mockery of not just what we believed, but what was *really* going on.

Julius is on the board right now, reading what people think, searching out others who might be ready to join us. The man has a mission, he's got drive, I'll give him that much. To tell you the truth, I mean, I wouldn't tell him this to his face, but he's a little odd. I tolerate it, though. It's nice to have company and being around someone else has given me the courage to travel outside.

"What did you hear?" he repeats.

"Oh, not much. Nothing really. They didn't say a word."

"Hmmph," he grunts. "Probably would have been speaking in Arabic anyway."

I nod my head. Odd or not, he usually knows what he's talking about.

"Anything new?" I ask, pointing at the computer. It's been at least three whole minutes since he's told me what he's reading, but I've run out of conversation. Frankly, I've grown a little tired of his constant updates. Hell, he's practically moved into my room on my dime, so he's gotten on my nerves in a lot of different ways.

"Nah, same jerks here," he says, pushing his hair back. Most of the time when people do that, it falls back down. His doesn't. It kind of just sticks there which freaks me out a little.

I look at Julius and try to figure out just what we're doing. Much of this year was quiet with Americans driving around waving their flags, being all patriotic. Every car had a flag decal, every house had Old Glory hanging out front, and *September 11, 2001, We Will Never Forget* was everywhere you turned your head.

Then one day it was gone. People got tired of taking their flag in and putting it back out. Decals faded. I will say, though, the memories didn't. People were still patriotic. They were still angry and remembering those we'd lost, they just weren't wearing it on their sleeves anymore.

The year was pretty quiet until a bombing at a Bali discotheque (yeah, I didn't know they still used that word either) killed two hundred people in October. A month and a half later, Al Qaeda bombed a resort in Kenya. They also fired a missile at a passenger jet, but luckily missed. Things were heating up again and Julius and I realized that these attacks, so far away, were just practice. They were keeping sharp, honing their skills, waiting for an opportunity to hit us on our home soil again. The two of us were determined not to be unprepared like last time.

While the terrorists have been off in their training camps, we've been doing some training of our own. We've studied their faces and we've studied what information we could find on their methods and tendencies. We've compared notes with other true patriots. We've learned how to build bombs and how to dismantle them. We've done our best to secure potassium iodide tablets for everyone who is prepared to fight the fight. If they're going to nuke us, we're going to be ready to protect ourselves.

Twice-weekly online meetings of the core group are what we've decided on. It seemed enough, but now we're in touch every day, learning, watching, and waiting. That's where we are.

Julius closes the laptop, stands up and stretches. Without a word, he throws his denim jacket around his shoulders and heads to the door.

"Wait, where are you going?" I ask, jumping up from my seat.

He stops, turns to me with a puzzled look on his face, and digs his pack of cigarettes out of his pocket.

"I'm going to have a smoke," he says. "No big deal."

I take a deep breath and nod. He leaves the room and I'm overwhelmed with envy at how easily he does it. He doesn't check the peephole. He doesn't listen at the door. Hell, I've tried to convince Julius that we should be armed, but so far he's managed to convince me it's not such a good idea.

After he's gone for about a minute, I go to the door and open it (checking the peephole first, of course). My key is somewhere in the room, so I open the latch to prevent the door from shutting just in case it slips from my grip. The hallway is empty and I can't help but wonder if Julius is going to return or not. Maybe he's tired of me. Maybe he thinks I'm a phony, too. And even if he doesn't think any of that, something terrible could happen to him while he's outside.

I start to walk down the hallway, intent on making sure that no harm comes to Julius, but the safety and security of the room beckons to me. I can just go back and wait in there for Julius to return. He'll come back in just a few minutes and I'll realize that all this worrying was for nothing. Two steps back toward the room and I stop.

No, I can't go back in there. Julius has been the only one who's believed in me and he could be downstairs in danger right now. He needs my help. I take a deep breath and grit my teeth. Then I force one foot in front of the other toward the elevator lobby, but of course I don't make it.

Damn! I think. *The door is still open.*

While I'm down saving Julius' life, the terrorists could sneak into my room and wait there to ambush me. At the very least, they could go in and bug the room or poison my food. They could even plant a dirty bomb. I mean, if they know I'm onto them, what *won't* they resort to?

I turn back toward the room and stop. Julius' life is at stake. I turn back toward the elevator. My heart is racing now and I'm beginning to sweat. I can't make up my mind. I bring my hands up to massage my temples but notice that I'm trembling uncontrollably. Even now, Julius could be lying dead in the street as a result of my indecision. What have I done? I've killed him and now he's gone forever.

I'm all alone again. I had someone I could relate to and I let it slip away. I ...

"Are you going to eat?"

I focus and glance toward the voice. It sounded like Julius, but that's impossible. He's dead in the street, right? Isn't he? Wait a minute, I thought—actually, I don't know what I thought. The voice came from the doorway of the room and when I look, there he is, holding a McDonald's bag. He must have walked right past me. He shakes the bag with a look on his face that says, *Yo, space cowboy, wake up and come eat.*

I look at my hands, which are still trembling, then back at Julius. When I don't respond, he tries again.

"Are you going to eat?"

Only, this time, it's not Julius. The voice is older, sweeter, feminine and it's coming from a distance. It's Aunt Beverly calling to me. I shake my head, trying to clear the images from my mind. Uncle Clint is sitting on the edge of the bed watching me, but I'm surprised at the look on his face. It's not humor. It's something much worse. It's pity.

I pick myself up off the floor and try to back out of the room as gracefully as possible. At least he seems to have forgotten about my eavesdropping.

"Don't think I forgot about the eavesdropping," he says.

Okay. So much for that.

"I catch you by that door again, I'll beat ya with the fire poker."

I give him two thumbs up as I back out the door.

"Got it," I say. "Fire poker."

I hate my life.

CHAPTER FIFTEEN

After my good, hearty (though slightly lukewarm) dinner, Uncle Clint arises from his "nap" and is privileged with a full sit-down meal. I can't help but wonder if either of them sees the problem with this. He comes home and gets in trouble, yet still gets waited on hand and foot. Aunt Beverly needs a little lesson on the women's movement. So does Uncle Clint for that matter. Apparently the only women's movement he knows is the one where they shake their ass on back to the kitchen to get him more food.

I avoid him as much as possible for the rest of the evening, though the brief moments when our paths cross are filled with icy glares that alternate between contempt and concern. I know it's killing him to find out what I overheard, so I keep it from him. Let him stew.

He's obviously trying to play it off like nothing happened, but I intend to find out exactly what's going on. I'll keep tabs on his phone calls, and listen in if I get the chance. In fact, I've already ...

Wait a second. This is insanity. What did I do? I run down the hallway to Uncle Clint's room and dive across his bedroom floor, sliding until I crash into the nightstand (thank God for well-polished hardwood). I grab my tape recorder out from under the bed and return just as quickly (and violently) to my room. Nobody has ever accused me of stealth.

I press the stop button on the tape recorder and peek out into the hallway just as Aunt Beverly calls out from the kitchen, "What in God's creation is that racket all about?"

"Nothing!" I assure her.

Luckily the hallway is empty. I close my bedroom door and collapse against it. What the hell was I thinking? A tape recorder! Who am I, Encyclopedia Brown? I smack the recorder against my head a few times to see which will give first.

Ow.

Rubbing my forehead, I look at the tape. More than half of it is used. I know I should erase it. I should rewind and just let it record nothing, but I can't. I mean, I rewind it. That part isn't the problem. The problem comes when my finger hits the *Play* button.

At first it's just a low hissing sound—the sound of silence. I'm telling myself that I shouldn't be listening to this, that it's just plain wrong. I think about how despicable the whole idea is as I listen to thirty minutes of blank tape.

My finger hovers above the stop button, ready to cede that I'd caught nothing, when I hear a couple of footsteps. Two. Three. They're heavy steps. It's definitely not Aunt Beverly. Some rustling, then a dresser drawer closes. More rustling.

This is captivating.

Wait. There's a click and some beeps. Is he dialing the phone? More silence. Come on, come on. If I shake this thing will he hurry up, damn it? I feel like he's never going to speak.

Then he does.

"Sorry about before," he whispers. "He was listening at the door."

A pause.

"I don't think he heard nothin'. He gave me some stupid smirk earlier tonight, like he wanted me to think he'd heard somethin'. That just means he didn't hear nothin'."

Damn, I knew I shouldn't have tried that smirk. This guy is smarter than he looks.

"Okay," he says, "see you soon."

I close my eyes as, behind my raging fury, a slight sensation of guilt begins to set in. I should be more worried about this private detective and his client, Matthew. There are things that happened—bad things—that could really come back to bite somebody. If Matthew is trying to reach me, if he really *is* one of the guys in our group, it can only mean things are falling apart. And if a private detective can get to Colorado Springs and find me in two days, the law will make it in half that time.

"They're ready, Jim."

I jump, thinking Uncle Clint found the tape recorder, but when I open my eyes Julius is holding my coat out to me. I stand up from my seat and take it from him.

"They there already?" I ask, trying desperately to remember just who "they" are and where "there" is.

"On their way. We should all get there about the same time."

I push my arm through the sleeve and find Julius still staring at me. He holds out his fist.

"You ready for this?" he asks. His brown eyes glisten with excitement, almost as much as his dark hair glistens with grease.

I hit his fist with mine.

"Let's do it," I say, all confusion gone from my mind.

He nods and we leave the hotel room. I stride down the hallway with confidence, not a trace of fear to be found. My chin is up and I'm pretty sure I don't blink until we get outside. Blinking is a sign of weakness and for what we're about to do, there can be none of that. Not an ounce.

Julius leads the way into the lot where we hop into his GMC Jimmy. This is one vehicle where the decals haven't faded. Attached to the antenna is a flag that gets replaced the moment there is a tear in it or the color begins to fade. In the CD player is a disc of patriotic songs.

On the way to our destination we listen to *Proud to be an American* by Lee Greenwood at least a half-dozen times. Oh, we don't just listen to it. We sing it. We belt it out. We're nice and loud until we approach the mall.

Pulling into the parking lot, Julius looks for the other cars, but I'm looking at the mall, itself: large, ornate, and full of people. Word on the street (and by street I mean message boards) is that the terrorists are going to attack our malls today.

Another attack on our home soil, on the very symbols of our capitalist society, and what do the American people do? They shop. Yup, they shop, they go to work, and they play. The government tells us to go about business as usual. Oh, no wait, to be fair they've raised the terrorist threat level. Well, that should do it, right? I can see it now: some Al Qaeda member riding in on an airplane, ready to use it as a bomb, ready to crash into a mall or a nuclear plant, but wait! Wait! Quick, turn the plane around. By Allah, turn it around! The threat level is up to orange! How could we have been so stupid?

I shake my head. Haven't we learned a thing? I look at the group of cars we're approaching and realize that maybe some of us have actually learned, just not as many as I'd like to see. Our team has parked toward the back of the aisles, but not so far back as to be conspicuous. Five cars with two to three people in each one. That should be enough to stop any terrorists. If nobody else is going to do it, I guess we will. We're enthusiastic, patriotic and smart.

Shit, I hope none of these idiots wore camouflage.

We park between a tough-as-nails Dodge Caravan and a bad-ass, crime-fighting Volkswagen Beetle. You can almost picture these manly vehicles with gun turrets. I glance at Julius who apparently has no problem saving the world with people who drive family-friendly vehicles and practical mid-size sedans. Not a single Hummer in the group or a tricked out pickup. Did I just say "tricked out"? Okay, just give me a pickup with a gun-rack. That's all I ask.

Julius looks at me. "Let's roll."

Oh, for the love of God, if that phrase hasn't been overused, call me Osama and shove a bunker-buster up my ... oh, never mind. Acting inspired, I leap from the car and bound around to the other side, ready for action. The others have already begun to emerge from their cars.

Great. The cars look tougher than their occupants.

Over the course of the next several minutes I am introduced to Phil the fast food restaurant manager, Sal the accountant, and a bunch of other non-descript people that kind of just blend together. One is named Matthew. I don't know why this is important, but for some reason it is. I try to remember their names, but it's a daunting task. A few of them look like Julius: unshaven and unclean. I think I would have been more comfortable with this had they all looked like that.

When the introductions are finished we all stand around looking at each other. We each wait for somebody else to tell us what to do. How do we find them? Do we go looking? Do we wait until something happens?

Nobody speaks.

I look down and kick a pebble. When that bores me, I watch a group of birds circling overhead. The wind is picking up and the birds seem to be working very hard just to stay in place. If they relax a wing for just a second, they get tossed and turned.

A woman walks by us with a baby in a stroller. You'd think she'd stare at such a band of jokers like us, but she doesn't. Nope, she does everything she can to avoid eye contact with us. I guarantee the moment she steps in through the doors of Sears she reports us to security.

Isn't that ironic? Not, of course in the Alannis Morrisette definition of ironic in which nothing is actually ironic, they just suck, but in the real sense. Here we are, feeling driven to action because of people's indifference. We are here to protect the citizens of America because they won't protect themselves. We're here because nobody is diligent enough to report suspicious activity to security. Yet we're going to be reported to security.

"Maybe we should go inside," I offer, watching the young mother pick up speed as she approaches the department store.

"Jim's right," Julius says. "We look like trouble out here. Let's set up some ground rules, some signals, things like that, then let's break up and get inside."

The group nods in unanimous approval. We spend a few minutes quickly going over the things Julius mentioned. Each time somebody passes us I get a little more worried. I start fidgeting and it's not long before Julius notices. He cuts short his little indoctrination into the He-man Terrorist Haters Club and urges us inside. We split up into groups of three. A pot-bellied, balding man joins Julius and me. This wouldn't be terrible except for the fact that he can't be more than twenty-three. At that age he should be physically fit, not balding and pot-bellied.

The mall appears more crowded than the amount of cars indicated. Damn public transportation. I scan the shoppers and notice one positive: it's midweek, so school has taken a large number of children out of the equation. There aren't many men, which is good and bad. It's bad because if things come to blows, I'm sure we'd love some helping hands. It's good because the fewer men there are, the easier it will be to spot terrorists in the crowd.

We stroll along the concourse, passing jewelry stores, clothing stores, and fancy coffee shops. We amble through the food court, noting every person eating a hamburger and crossing them off our mental checklists. Our sector of the mall covered, we pull up seats in front of Wendy's.

Julius' phone chirps.

"Go ahead," he says.

"Sector five clear," the voice on the other end says.

Julius flips open his phone to take the voice off speaker.

"10-4," he whispers. The phone beeps four more times. Each sector, including ours, is clear. Terry, our pot-bellied buddy, gets up to get us some sodas.

"What do you think?" I ask Julius.

He doesn't answer.

"Julius?"

"Shh."

I freeze. He sees something and I don't want to look around and give it away.

After a few more moments of silence, he whispers, "Terrorist. Three o'clock."

I try to get a look with my peripheral vision but the suspect is just out of sight. I lean back in my chair and pretend to stretch. There he is. Julius is right. Middle-Eastern without a doubt. This is our man.

The phone is back in hand.

"We've got one," Julius whispers.

Terry returns with our drinks and we do our best to fill him in on the situation, but when he isn't able to decipher our pantomime, we give up and tell him we'll fill him in later. After a few minutes, the terrorist gets up and walks away. We let him reach the end of the food court before we follow.

Keeping a good twenty yards behind, I notice the neatly pressed khaki pants, his stylish yellow button down, and his Italian shoes (I imagine they're Italian, though I can't distinguish Italian from Iowan when it comes to shoes). Halfway to the escalator, another Middle-Eastern man exits a bookstore and joins the one we are following. They speak a few words to each other, then continue on in silence. Neither is carrying a shopping bag.

The terrorists step onto the escalator and, while they descend, we are joined by three of our colleagues. I look over the guardrail and find two more of our teams waiting below. This is good. We've got them covered.

Rather than follow directly, we let our colleagues pick up the tail. They keep us informed via cell phone and we take a more roundabout route to where they are headed. By the time the two men hit the parking lot, we are what can only be described as an angry mob. One of the terrorists looks back over his shoulder and sees us. His panic is visible, even from this distance.

"Damn it," Julius growls, "we've been spotted."

How could we not be? How often do grown men go to malls in groups of fifteen?

The terrorist who spotted us says something to his partner. They've got approximately a twelve parking space lead on us at the moment, but they break into a run, gaining at least another six spaces before any of us can get our feet moving. They get to their car and hurriedly climb in, but we descend upon them like birds of prey finding their first meal in weeks. Julius gets his hand on the car door before the driver-side terrorist can get it closed.

I'm completely caught up in all this. There's yelling and hooting and downright craziness. Julius pulls the driver from his car and the passenger-side terrorist hops out to assist his friend. So far, no weapons have been drawn, but something nags at the back of my mind that we probably already knew there would be no weapons involved. It's a voice of reason in my head that says what we are doing is wrong because we have no reason to believe that these men are terrorists, yet I manage to silence it. That's lunacy talking and I can't be distracted.

Both men are pressed by their throats to the car while a mob of angry men hurls questions and accusations at them.

"Thought you could do it again?" one of us yells.

"What did you do, plant a bomb?" somebody else yells. It may have even been me.

"Is it a dirty bomb?"

"A biological attack?"

The questions begin to blend together. We're all yelling at once and I can feel the heat rising in me. My muscles tense. One of the two men we've got cornered is shaking, the other appears to just be in shock.

"What have we done?" the shorter man yells. "We are not terrorists. We love America."

His protests are cut short by a sharp slap as Julius smacks him across the mouth.

"Don't you ever dishonor this country like that again."

The nervous one keeps asking what they've done and begging us to leave them alone, but Julius insists they've planted bombs or biological agents in the mall.

One of the men announces that he is an American citizen and can prove it. He reaches for his pocket, but Julius stops him by punching him in the stomach with such force that the man doubles over. When that happens, Julius embraces the opportunity to thrust a knee into the man's face. The terrorist collapses to the ground, blood pouring from his nostrils. Passenger-side terrorist begins to pray to Allah.

"Shut yer frickin' mouth," one of our members yells, then punches him across the jaw. Suddenly, I lose my animal instinct. I look at the scene before me and I'm physically ill. Fists and feet are flying and a steel blade suddenly gleams in the daylight, then arcs outward. Unfortunately, I haven't moved far enough away and the blade slices a deep cut into the back of my hand.

"Fuck!" I scream, pressing the back of my hand to my shirt and retreating to Julius' truck. I can feel the blood start to gush. Back in the melee, the two Middle-Eastern men are curled up on the cold asphalt trying to do anything they can to protect themselves.

It's not until Julius' steel-toed boot crashes into the temple of the driver-side victim with an audible crunch that the kicking and punching stops. We all watch in horror as the man's body falls limp. Julius looks at me with panic in his eyes, or maybe it's excitement. He's bouncing now, still filled with testosterone and adrenaline. His body is trying to flee in ten different directions, but he finally gains control. The second man is unconscious but we're pretty sure the first is far worse than that.

"Go!" Julius insists. "Go!"

Everybody scrambles. I dive into Julius' car and he's screeching out of the parking space before I can even close my door. It leaves a long dent and scratch the length of the Dodge Caravan. We rocket out of the parking lot, ignoring stop signs and weaving in and out of traffic. The entire time I'm staring at Julian with disgust.

"Here, hold this!" he says, thrusting the knife in my direction. "I must have cut one of those camel-jockeys. It's got blood all over it."

"That's my blood, asshole," I holler through gritted teeth.

He looks at me, then back at the road without saying a word or offering an apology.

What the hell have I gotten myself into?

All I can do is pray we were not caught on surveillance video. There is also a remote hope that these men really have planted some kind of bomb at the mall. At least that way we'd be justified. I want to lash out at Julius, but for now, I know I need to work with him. Pissing him off would only give him a great scapegoat for this afternoon's debacle.

I put my chin down to my chest and …

CLICK.

I snap my head up, but I'm no longer looking at the interior of Julius' car. Instead, I'm looking at the inside of my bedroom in Aunt Beverly's house and the recorder in my hand has come to the end of the tape. I'm not sure if it held any more incriminating evidence and I'm not sure I want to know.

That incident on that terrible day is a number of years ago now, but it still haunts me like it happened yesterday. I shudder as a chill runs the length of my spine.

"Please forgive me, God," I whisper, to a deity in which I'm not even sure I believe.

Chapter Sixteen

I'm sitting on a stool at a drawing table tilted to a forty-five degree angle (not me, the table, though I do feel a bit off-kilter). On it are sheets of blank paper, various colors of paint and markers, some pens and pencils, and brushes. It's all the stuff I need to create a masterpiece. These materials coupled with the troubled thoughts that gallivant through my head should make for world-renowned art.

Yet, the pages are blank.

I pick up a brush, then set it down. Maybe paint isn't the medium I want to work with tonight. I pick up some charcoal, then put that back down as well. Nothing feels right. My mind keeps going back and forth between Uncle Clint's conversation on the tape and memories of that day in the mall parking lot. I want to forget about them both, but I can't bring myself to do that. Aunt Beverly's honor is at stake and I won't sit idly by and let Uncle Clint destroy her. At the same time, going to prison for the rest of my life is up there on my list of things I didn't want to do before I died.

I pick up a number six pencil, then put it down. The artwork is supposed to help me. When I first discussed with Dr. Wallace how tortured I was feeling the nights after my sessions, he suggested I give myself an outlet for my emotions. He told me to bring my work to the following session and we could discuss its implications. To this point I've never brought a piece of my art to his office, but he had been deadly accurate about how much better it would make me feel.

Aunt Beverly recognized the positive effects the art had on me, so she didn't hesitate to buy a drawing table. I sit at it at least three times a week now, sometimes even four or five. I think about how my flash-backs had gone away, but have now come back and, of course, the phrase that immediately comes to mind is, *back to the drawing board.*

It's late and the house is quiet. I think about Uncle Clint lying there next to Aunt Beverly and I cringe. Can she be as naïve to this whole sit-uation as she seems to be, or is it me? On the other hand, is there no situation at all except one which my paranoid mind is creating? Maybe Uncle Clint is just being secretive because he's tired of me poking my nose into his business.

I scratch a few lines onto a piece of paper with a pencil, but they're not forming anything. No portrait, no landscape, no still-life to repre-sent my hatred or fear. Heck, right now I'd even take a painting of a spilled-over basket of fruit that could show me my resentment of my father and love of my mother. At least I'd know there was something inside working its way out.

Normally, I'd have no problem creating some artwork after a session with Dr. Wallace, but the truth is, I've had this flashback about the mall before and each time it leaves me numb. That was a low point in my life and I have never forgiven myself for the atrocities in which I participated. At times, I've wrestled with the idea of going back and turning myself in, but that would only lead to the destruction of twelve or thirteen other lives—lives of guys who just found themselves knee-deep in something they didn't fully understand. Each time the thought of confession arises, I use the lives of the other men as my excuse to not follow through.

I lay the pencil down and get up from the stool. Pacing the room, I'm tortured with images of that day. I can see the faces of the two men and the horror we caused. I can still hear Julius' boot crunch into the man's skull. We were the terrorists that day, not them.

I pick the pencil back up and put it to paper. "We were the terrorists," I mutter as I drag the graphite across the paper. I tilt the pencil on its side to add a shadow to an angle. I don't know what the angle is or why it needs a shadow, but I trust my hand knows what it's doing. "We were the terrorists," I insist. It has become my mantra.

Scratch, scratch, scratch goes the pencil against the paper.

Mantra.

Scratch, scratch, scratch.

Mantra.

Before long, this pattern has created a form on the paper. It is a face—a ragged looking man with long, greasy hair. There's no mistaking who it is. He was a part of my life for such a brief period of time, in all relativity, but he had such an impact—as destructive an impact as a steel-toed boot on bone.

I'm amazed at how detailed the picture is. It's been quite a bit of time since I last saw Julius, yet there it is, every last hair on his head, every bit of stubble, every pimple or ingrown hair right there on my paper. His eyes are dull and grey, partly because it's a pencil drawing, but partly because that's how I see Julius in my mind: lifeless.

I stare at the drawing, studying each wrinkle in his face. There are even a few nose-hairs poking out from his nostrils. As I look at that face that led me down one of the darkest paths of my existence, I feel the pull of a flashback. For some reason, this one doesn't sneak up on me. I begin to fight the pull, but in the back of my mind I know I have to go. I have to complete the cycle or I'll never be right. One last look at Julius' face and I let myself go …

… only to find myself looking right at Julius' face.

Sweat is trickling down from his brow so consistently it looks like one of those panes of glass you can get at a novelty store that always look like its raining on the other side. His hair is clinging to his face, like it's starving for grease and it's hoping to lap it up off of his cheeks and forehead. Every once in a while I find myself staring at a clump of hair, waiting to see if it will move on its own, convinced that it's more tentacle than it is hair.

Over Julius' shoulder is a mirror and I can see that, despite maybe not being washed as often as it should be, my hair looks a hell of a lot better than his does. With Julius around, I find that I take a little bit better care of myself. I'm not up to pre-9/11 standards by any means, but I'm looking a little less scary if I do say so myself.

My eyes drift away from my reflection to the two wallet-sized photos wedged into the mirror's frame. One is of Rebecca and me on a ski trip. The other is a picture of Andrew. It's a school shot at least a year out of date by now. Every time I see it, I fear that it is the last picture I will ever see of him. My heart sinks each time I think that memories of my son will be frozen in a forced, gap-toothed smile. His hair is a mess, certainly not the way his mother sent him off to school that day, and he is wearing a turtleneck and a sweater in which he seems anything but comfortable. Nevertheless, it is a photo of him and I use it as a stepping stone to other memories, so I'll never forget what he looks like.

"That was wild!" Julius says, awakening me from my daydream. He's sterilizing a needle in the flame of his lighter and holding my hand to the table, palm down.

I study him for a moment, praying that he's referring to something other than what just occurred at the mall, but from what I can see there can be nothing else. His hands are shaking so much it's a wonder he can hold the needle in the flame long enough to heat it up. If I saw him on the street, I'd insist he was high on cocaine. But I know better. I know that drugs are not what he's high on.

I want to say that it wasn't wild, it was wrong, but I can't. He'll tear me to pieces. He'll accuse me of siding with our enemy. He'll tell me I've become weak, which I know I haven't. I still loathe these people, but random murder? I can't deal with that. The problem is, I don't want Julius to think I'm going to turn him in. If he believes that, he might resort to something awful. My skull could be the next recipient of his steel-toed boot. At the very least, I'll get jabbed with a red-hot needle.

"I mean, we stopped those motherfuckers, man. We're goddamned heroes," he says as he begins to stitch me up.

I'm trying to distract myself from the pain by watching him and he doesn't even appear to believe his own words. It's like he's trying to convince himself, not me. The words are there, meaningless, insincere, but that doesn't matter, he'll believe them and then we'll be off on another mission. Worrying about when he'll come to that conclusion bothers me almost as much as the threat of terrorism does.

Finished with his hack job, he gets up from his seat and paces the room, stopping every so often to peel back the heavy drapes and look out the window. He's told me repeatedly how we've gotten off scott-free, but he still continues to look to make sure the authorities aren't pulling up outside.

I close my eyes and lean back in the chair, rubbing my throbbing hand, but the faces of the men in the parking lot seem to hover just behind my eyelids, so my eyes don't stay closed very long. It's at that moment, while Julius is executing a military-like about-face at the far end of the room, that I come up with a reason to support the actions my conscience has been urging me toward.

With no internal debate, I blurt out, "We have to turn ourselves in."

Julius stops. His eyes close and his chin drops to his chest, causing the greasy mop on his head to flop down around his face.

"Oh, tell me I didn't just hear that," he mutters.

"Listen to me, Julius," I say, nearly with excitement as I gain momentum. "The other one. The other guy. Something's been nagging at me since we got back and that's what it is."

"The other guy," he states, sitting down across from me at the small table.

It's not a question. Julius is a smart guy. He's made the connection already. I can see the cogs and gears cranking away already in his mind.

"Yes, the other guy. Since we got back all you've been doing is going over how smoothly this went," I continue, trying not to inflect any of the words with sarcasm, "but it didn't. There are loose ends. You said there were no witnesses. That couldn't be further from the truth."

Julius takes the pack of Camels from his pocket, smacks it against his palm a few times, and removes one from the pack. He plays with it for a while before finally putting it in his mouth and lighting it. I don't know why I remain silent through all this, but I feel it's what I need to do.

The smoke from the cigarette rises around his head, though not like a wreath. Instead, it reaches up and engulfs him like the licks of flame on a witch's execution pyre. He stands up from the chair and paces away. After two steps he stops and suddenly turns.

"You're absolutely right," he says.

"Good," I reply, exhaling a breath I'd apparently been holding in. "We can gather up the guys …"

"No, not about that. Not about that."

Now I'm scrambling. I don't know what he's referring to, but I know it can't be any good.

"The other guy. He's a loose end. You're right about that," he continues, staring off into the far corner of the room.

"Right, so we turn ourselves in. Tell the police it was an accident."

He brings his gaze to meet mine. "Are you out of your fuckin' mind? I will not bring myself to apologize for *anything* I do to these miserable bastards."

He sits back down, still with a look of incredible concentration.

"Besides, they'd never believe it," he mumbles.

"Well what other choice do we have?" I ask, the tone of my voice rising just a little higher than I would have liked. Before the question even finishes escaping my lips, I know that I don't want to hear Julius' answer.

"Just one, as far as I can tell."

He takes a long draw on his cigarette then blows the smoke out through his nostrils. We're locked in a staring contest right now. First one to blink loses. In other words, if I blink, we go murder another man. If he blinks, we still go murder another man, but Julius is forced to face the mean reality that he can't beat me in a staring contest. Having a backbone right about now would be nice.

He flips open the laptop and begins typing a message. My mind is screaming out to stop him, to tell him that he can't do this, but maybe I'm hoping one of the other guys will be the voice of reason.

"Looks like everybody was just waiting to hear from me," he says. "They're in."

"They're in?"

"Yeah, why? Aren't you?"

I want to say no, but I can't. It doesn't matter either way. Before I can answer, Julius brings his face to mine. He tries to lock eyes with me again, but I can't bring myself to look at him. For some reason, I feel ashamed.

"Listen closely," he whispers. There is no doubt from those two words alone that what is about to follow is a threat. "We've got a problem here. One you were gracious enough to point out. If it wasn't for that, we could have found ourselves in some deep shit. Therefore, I'm going to let your uneasiness slide a little bit, but there's no room for doubt in this world anymore, soldier. No room."

His breath is stale with smoke and his spit showers my face as he makes his point. My eyes remain lowered, but I find myself nodding.

"Good," he says, in reaction to my nod, "because as long as we're all in, we're good. Right?"

I nod again. My hands want to jump from my side to grab my head and hold it motionless.

"I mean, if somebody were to jump ship, how could we ever trust him again? That, in my opinion, would be the kind of guy that would need to take the fall for what happened, don't you agree?"

I can no longer even nod. My spirit is broken. I've brought myself to this place and now I have to pay the consequences. Whatever Julius wants, Julius gets. I bring my eyes up and stare into his face: the stubble, the wrinkle by his eyes, the acne on his neck, a couple of pockmarks on his cheeks, and those cold, dead grey eyes.

I stare at the eyes for a minute, then they seem to go flat. I blink, clear my vision, and look again, but nothing has changed. They are flat and grey, but so is the rest of Julius.

I grab the piece of paper off the drawing board and crumple the portrait. I turn to throw it in the waste basket, but I can't. Instead, I flatten it out and try to smooth as many wrinkles as possible. No matter how much I hate Julius, I can't deny how good it felt to have someone in my life who understood what I was going through. I look at the picture one final time before opening the cover of my drawing tablet. I place the portrait inside on a stack of five or six other loose sheets of paper, each one bearing the same picture of Julius' face.

CHAPTER SEVENTEEN

Often, with nighttime comes depression. Actually, I'm depressed all the time, but nighttime is the worst. It's got something to do with the sunshine producing more serotonin in my body. At least, that's what they tell me. I just know it sucks during the day and sucks more at night. I always thought it was because another day was coming to a close in which I hadn't gotten any better, which meant another was about to begin in which I'd need to go through the same miserable existence. To-may-to, to-mah-to.

My recent string of flashbacks isn't helping much, either. I really wish Aunt Beverly was awake so I could talk to somebody about this, but she's not and I wouldn't disturb her just so I could feel better. I wander around the house trying to find something to occupy my time, but nothing seems to grab my attention. Television seems boring and my artwork is through for the night. I'm starting to think that a video game system might be in order. At least it would offer me an escape from reality.

I drag my ass into the bathroom and open the medicine cabinet. When I first moved in, Aunt Beverly had stripped this baby bare. I couldn't even find a single ibuprofen if I needed one. I had to ask her for one and she would get it for me (and watch me take it to ensure I wasn't stockpiling them for a future overdose). Truth is, that was never even an option, not when I lost my wife and son, not when I participated in killing a man, not ever. Maybe it should have been.

I close the medicine cabinet, which has since been restocked, and study my face in the mirror. In five years I've aged ten. I still look better than Julius ever did, though. I guess that counts for something.

I run the cold water and splash some on my face, hoping it will invigorate me in some way. When it doesn't, I head for the family room where Aunt Beverly keeps her collection of books. Maybe something in there can keep my mind off things.

I stand in front of the bookcase, scanning the titles on the spines. I need something with grit, something with feeling. I need something to break me out of this funk, whether it is side-splitting comedy or extreme gratuitous violence. I need emotion. Then a title catches my eye.

Slaughterhouse Five, by Kurt Vonnegut.

Now, that sounds violent.

I pull the book off the shelf and look at the cover. I turn it sideways. Not too thick, that's a bonus. I open it up and begin to read the flap:

Billy Pilgrim has become unstuck in time.

I read the rest of the synopsis which tells me that Billy Pilgrim jumps around to different moments in his life, unable to control when or where he's going to land. The book sounds interesting enough, not violent like I'd hoped, but interesting. Something about that first sentence, though, keeps haunting me.

Billy Pilgrim has become unstuck in time.

That's exactly how I feel: unstuck in time.

I sit down in Aunt Beverly's mahogany Victorian armchair and open to the first page of the story (Uncle Clint doesn't have a chair in the library area of the family room, in fact, the only thing he's been known to ever read is *Farm Journal* while on the toilet). The chair is narrow and the upholstery isn't exactly comfortable. I shift and fidget, trying to find that perfect position, but it's impossible. The only way to sit in this chair is the way Aunt Beverly sits in it: looking straight ahead and with perfect posture.

So, I try it her way. I place my feet on the floor and keep my back straight. I hold the book up to eye-level, but I can't keep from fidgeting. Suddenly it's not a Victorian armchair that's making me uncomfortable, it's the front seat of a GMC Jimmy.

I glance around to get my bearings and I see Julius driving the vehicle. He's hunched over the wheel, steering the car with his arms instead of his hands. His eyes stare at the road ahead and he never seems to blink. He's got a cigarette between his lips, but it's not lit.

He still hasn't told me his plan, which makes me even more nervous than does simply being here. I shift in my seat, tug at the seatbelt, and adjust my shirt. I lower the window a little bit to get some fresh air, but the temperature dipped to near-freezing once the sun went down, so I quickly close it.

"Relax," Julius says, the cigarette sticking to his lower lip. "We'll do this and there will be nobody left to turn on us."

I nod, unconvinced. The streets are racing by us and I can't help but wonder if we'll be able to make it to our destination without being stopped by the police or wrapping ourselves around a telephone pole. Considering the alternative—successfully completing the task Julius has set out to perform—the telephone pole isn't looking half-bad right now.

"Where, exactly, are we going?" I ask. "You don't know this guy or where he lives. How do you expect to find him?"

"First we meet up with the other guys. Once we're all together, we stake out the police department. The guy still has to be there. When he's done, no matter how long that takes, we follow him home and take care of things there."

He pulls the wheel hard to the left, making me crash into my door. We fishtail a bit, but he regains control and we rocket on down the street. A block later, he pulls to the curb and shuts the engine off.

I assume this is where we're supposed to meet the others, but there is nobody around. It's a quiet suburban neighborhood with million-dollar homes. I don't know how Julius knows about this neighborhood and I really don't want to know, but it seems to me that we'd actually be pretty conspicuous here in our GMC Jimmy, meeting up with Volkswagon Beetles and Dodge minivans.

Julius must have noticed my discomfort with our location. "I figured there was no chance anybody here would recognize any of us," he snickers.

Once again, I'd underestimated him.

Within minutes, Julius becomes just as fidgety as me. He checks his watch every thirty seconds and mumbles something that sounds hostile. After about thirty time-checks, he slams the heel of his hand into the steering wheel repeatedly.

"Damn, damn, damn, damn, damn!"

I wait for his tirade to end before I let myself think about the implications. His outburst means he thinks the other guys aren't going to show up. That, in itself, is great; maybe he's going to abort his mission. Maybe the other guys had the nerve to do what I didn't: save a man's life.

"What's the next move?" I ask, hoping to hear him say we'll turn around and head back to the hotel.

He takes a deep breath and sits for a moment with his head resting on the steering wheel. Without lifting it, he replies, "I guess it's just us."

The statement makes me shudder. He still hasn't changed his mind. What the hell would it take to get this guy to realize that we're defeated?

"You can't be serious," I say. "You want us to go there alone, sit outside a *police station*, and follow a man whose friend we just murdered a few hours ago."

"Shut your mouth," Julius hisses.

"No. No, Julius, I won't shut my mouth."

"I'm warning you, Jim. Shut your mouth or I'll shut it for you."

Nothing is stopping me now. My momentum is going to carry me through this argument.

"Warn me all you want, but you need to face reality here. We're alone. We've got the smallest of hopes that we can literally get away with murder, but there's no way we can get away with two. No way."

He starts the engine and pulls the car away from the curb. "We don't have a choice."

"Yes we do!"

"No, we don't. We're going to do this. It's the only way. Besides, Jim, he's a terrorist. When did you go so soft?"

"How do you know that? Just because he's from the Middle-East? Tell me what country."

"What?"

"Tell me what country. Is he from Jordan? Iraq? Israel? Saudi Arabia?"

"I don't know. What does it matter?"

We're speeding through the streets of Fort Lee again, heading toward the police station. I need to break through; I need to get him to realize his mistake before it's too late to turn back.

"It matters because we don't know a thing about this guy or his friend for that matter."

"Who cares? They're all terrorists, all of them!"

"No they're not!" I scream.

Julius continues on with his argument, but I'm no longer listening. All I can hear is my last statement ringing in my ears. My God, what have I been doing? I've been so afraid for my life that I've turned everyone into the enemy.

Before long we pull into a parking spot about a half block away from the police station. Julius is staring at me with eyes of coal that once fueled a fire long since extinguished. I'm assuming from his gaze that he's waiting for a response to a question he's posed, but I didn't hear it so I just wait without speaking.

This apparently frustrates him and I find myself staring down the barrel of a gun. I'd mention the type, but when you're looking down a barrel, you realize just how unimportant that detail is. From this range, they'd pretty much all do the same damage.

Just about now, I'm really wishing I'd been paying attention to what he asked me. I feel my hands begin to tremble. The gun is also trembling, but I can't tell if that's because Julius is shaking or because I'm shaking.

"You lousy coward," he spits. "Get the fuck outta my car."

At this point, I don't care what he asked me, I know an opportunity to avoid getting a bullet in my head when I see one. I reach for the door handle, fumble with it, then fall out of the car more than exit it under my own mechanics.

When I stand up and look back into the car, Julius has lowered the gun. He looks at me with defeat. The look communicates one word and one word only: betrayal.

"Where did you get that?" I manage, nodding at the gun. "You said no weapons."

"I said none for you. Just go."

I back away, but not because I think he'll shoot me, it's because I hope to catch one last opportunity to stop him. If I can just see a moment of doubt on his face, I could take advantage of it, but there is no indication that he's anything but determined to carry out his task.

I continue on down the sidewalk until I see somebody coming down the front steps of the police department. I squint to get a better look to confirm my initial reaction: it's the man from the mall. I watch as he is escorted to a police car by a uniformed officer and, until I watch Julius follow them away, I have a remote amount of hope that this will be enough of a deterrent.

A few paces down the sidewalk, I take a seat on a wooden bench. Watching the people pass by, the New Jersey Transit buses stop and depart, and shoppers peruse window displays, it is not long before I am reminded of just how alone I am. Julius is gone. Bad influence or not, he was my cornerstone for most of the past year.

I suddenly find myself short of breath. I want to get up from the bench, but I don't know how I'd get anywhere; I am too afraid to take a bus or a taxi and my feet seem immobile. I shift on the bench, trying to find a position of some comfort, but it's impossible. This bench is as uncomfortable as ...

... Aunt Beverly's chair, which is actually what I'm sitting on. I glance around the room and shake off the haziness of the flashback. In my hands rests a closed copy of Slaughterhouse Five. I never even got to read the first paragraph.

By now, sleep has begun to get its tantalizing grip on me, but I can't push the image of a GMC Jimmy heading down the street in pursuit of a police car out of my head. That was the last time I ever saw Julius. Eventually, my fear of being exposed out in public overrode my fear of public transportation and I took my chances on a bus back to the hotel. Normally, that would have drained me to exhaustion, but my fear that Julius would come back to exact some sort of twisted revenge on me or to frame me for the murders added to my momentum. I packed my bags and left the hotel as quickly as possible without a destination in mind.

I stand up from Aunt Beverly's chair, vowing never to sit in it again. I return the book to the shelf and tell myself, somewhat convincingly, that I'll read it another time. For now, I'm off to brush my teeth and try to get what is undoubtedly some well-deserved shut-eye.

CHAPTER EIGHTEEN

When I wake to the sound of geese honking outside my window, I take a moment to thank God that I've managed to sleep through the night (I may not believe, but some habits die hard). Sometimes, even getting up to go to the bathroom can mean I'm awake through the next day. A younger, less embittered version of me would have stayed there to enjoy the comfort of the bed and the peaceful sounds of the great outdoors, but the new me can't be bothered.

I get up and go to the kitchen to make myself a bowl of oatmeal only to encounter Uncle Clint in the middle of one of his secret phone conversations. I guess I'm lucky he still believes that cordless phones are "the devil's tools" otherwise I might not have caught him in the act. He quickly hangs up the phone, which seems to be the new standard operating procedure each time I enter a room. I look at him, sigh, and shake my head. He glares at me in return, his entire face flushed the color of a slab of raw beef. It's good to see that our relationship hasn't improved any, but truthfully, I'm done with this. Today, I need to tell Aunt Beverly what I know; he's acting suspiciously and she deserves to be told. I'm positive this is beyond my usual paranoia. So far, he's been lucky that I've been the one to walk in on his conversations, but sooner or later it will be Aunt Bev and that will crush her.

No words are spoken between us, but we are thinking so loudly at each other that I'm sure Aunt Beverly will soon yell at us from the other room to shut our mental traps. She doesn't, though, and instead comes into the room armed with a half-dozen ratty, old duffle bags.

"Goodwill time," she says, throwing a few of them to each of us. "Fill 'em up and don't be shy. There's good people out there who can't afford what you're feeding to the moths."

She's got a great heart, but I own a total of three shirts and a whopping two pair of pants. It will be slim picking.

"I see that look on your face, James. It's time you parted with some of those juvenile t-shirts of yours—you know, the ones with all those rock and roll singers."

Check that. It looks like she's going to need to get me a few more duffle bags. I groan my discontent and storm out of the room, ruffling her hair as I pass by to let her know I'm teasing her. Behind me I hear her threaten Uncle Clint with a 'whoopin' if he doesn't get moving, just before he follows me, defeated, down the hall.

The separation will do us both some good, but I'm sure he's stewing over my behavior as much as I'm stewing over his. I kneel before my dresser and pull open the overstuffed t-shirt drawer. The main piles are folded fairly neatly, but after that every available gap is jammed with another shirt.

I stare at them for a minute, trying to figure out how I'm possibly supposed to part with my U2 concert shirts and the classic Pubs of Ireland t-shirt I've had since college. Eventually, fearing Aunt Beverly's wrath, I begin indiscriminately stuffing them into the bag. It's like pulling a bandage off a wound: if you do it real fast it's not supposed to hurt, but that's a load of bull and it still ends up stinging like mad. I feel like the only part of my past I still have is on its way to Goodwill.

One t-shirt after another gets pushed into the bag until there is no room left. I reach for another duffle, but my hand comes away empty; the pile is gone. Confused, I look back to the drawer to see if I accidentally put them in there with the remaining shirts, but the drawer is now completely empty.

Before I even look into my bag, I know I will find more than just t-shirts; I'll find it overflowing with jeans, flannel shirts, underwear and socks. I know that when I look up I will not find the feminine floral patterns of Aunt Beverly's guest room, but rather the dull earth-tones of a Fort Lee, New Jersey hotel room. In the time it takes to lift my head, all thoughts of Goodwill are replaced by fears of Bad-Julius.

One quick glance around the room shows that the only thing I've left behind is Julius' computer. I contemplate taking it with me, but I quickly realize the wealth of incriminating evidence that must be on the hard drive. If that's the case, and if Julius is successful with his "mission", he'd have good reason to come after me. No, the laptop stays and, with it, hopefully any future interaction with that maniac.

With no emotion or nostalgia, I leave the room for the last time. I don't bid it good riddance and I don't destroy anything on the way out. My concentration is focused solely on keeping one foot in front of the other. I try to distract myself by singing a song in my head, but I relentlessly end up back on *Proud to be an American* which reminds me not only of Julius, but also of who my original enemy is. When the singing fails, I try to play a game like counting all the people wearing red, but that soon turns into "Count the Arabs." The good thing is: I'm so busy trying to find new ways to distract myself that I'm already aboard a bus to south Jersey before I realize that nothing is working.

The doors hiss closed while I'm still standing in the aisle. It's not that I can't find a seat, it's that I'm actually frozen in place. The bus is only half-filled, but every face aboard is staring at me. It's probably not too strange to see somebody standing on a bus, but I'm pretty sure the look on my face right now is fairly amusing to somebody who's not experiencing the same crippling fear I am.

I force my leg to move, expecting it to sever itself from my foot which I know to be frozen to the floor of the bus. The crunch of breaking bone is expected, but it doesn't come. This is encouraging, so I force my other foot ahead. The other passengers seem to watch me with a blend of apprehension and amusement. My movements rival those of Frankenstein's monster, though the look on my face is probably more akin to Igor. I suddenly find myself thinking that a mob of villagers with pitchforks and torches would be merciful at this point. Two old ladies squeeze close together as I pass their seat and another woman gives me an icy glare that tells me with no ambiguity that I am not to sit with her. I'm starting to feel like the kid on the school bus that nobody likes and I won't be surprised if someone pelts me in the forehead with a Milk Dud.

The bus rumbles forward and bounces over a speed bump. Sure that the sudden motion is the beginning of an explosion, I throw my arms in front of my face while making a futile attempt to suppress a scream. People are now sliding as close to their windows as possible and, out of the corner of my eye, I notice a few people behind me shift to seats closer to the door. I finally manage to plant myself into an empty row where I let out a deep sigh of relief. Unfortunately, nobody else seems to experience the same relief. They're all watching me now without looking directly at me. All except for the bus driver who is staring so intently at me in the rear-view mirror that I can't imagine how he's managing to keep the bus on the road.

I slide over to the window, but one glance outside at the industrial vista of the New Jersey Turnpike and I'm back to the aisle seat. Outside is nothing but oil refineries, airports, bridges, and heavy traffic: too many targets. I feel my heart racing like it does after I've had way too much salt and a dull thumping is developing behind my eyes. Sweat is pooling in my armpits and my shirt has become noticeably stained.

I start glancing around the bus in a twitchy, jerky manner. I can't help it. I just need to look from one face to another. I need to know that they're not conspiring against me. It's getting really hot on the bus. For the love of God, I wish the driver would put the heat down. Maybe he's trying to sweat me out. I'm not leaving. I won't get off his bus. I've got to get far, far away from the city. I no longer have Julius to ground me. I'm alone, alone, all alone. I'm vulnerable to attack. This bus could be rigged to explode. Maybe it is. Maybe I should get off. But if I get off the bus, what will I do? I'm not taking a cab. No way. They're all terrorists.

A small boy stares at me and I wonder, with awe, how the enemy has managed to recruit and brainwash such young children. Even women have become suicide bombers. Is that this boy's plan? I stare back at him. Something in the back of my mind tells me to leave him alone, but what if that's what all the people who saw the 9/11 terrorists before the attack did? What if they all listened to their inner voices and left them alone?

I consider getting up to disarm him, but once again I can't move. I look at the boy's blond hair and blue eyes and think about how crafty the enemy has become. Breathing has become a chore. Shallow, rapid breaths are all I can manage. The boy seems to sense my disgust with him, but I'm not sure if he turns around on his own or at his mother's bidding. How despicable. She'll sacrifice her own child by strapping a bomb to him. I could kill them both if I could just move.

No, I can't kill them. Then I've become Julius. Maybe I'm wrong. Maybe they're not terrorists. Maybe I'm safe.

Impossible. Nobody's safe. Safety is an illusion.

I grab my hair in both fists and rock in the seat trying to slow my brain down for just one minute. When that doesn't work, I smack my head into the back of the seat in front of me.

"Damn you, Julius," I mumble. He's left me alone and I hate him for it.

"Why did you leave me?" I continue. "I hate you."

My quiet rant has gotten a little louder. I look up to see if anyone heard me and, apparently, everyone did. The bus driver is speaking something quietly into his radio. I want to shut up now, but for some reason my mouth continues to work on its own.

"You left me by myself. I didn't want to leave," I insist. "I didn't leave. I'm alone. You left."

I taste tears on my lips as I hiss my angry tirade.

"All I needed was somebody to help me. I just needed somebody to be there for me. You left."

People are literally cringing away from me now and I can't understand why I won't shut up.

"Why?" I cry. "Why did you leave me alone?"

The pace of my rocking increases, but instead of smacking my head into the seat, I'm looking into the faces of the other passengers. They're terrified. I'm terrified. They're whispering to one another, comforting each other, but I've got nobody to comfort me.

"Why did you leave me all by myself?" I yell. "Why did you take my son?"

The whispers stop and through a few of the frightened glances, I think I might actually see pity. The words that I've just hollered finally register in my mind and my rocking stops. Suddenly, everything is painted with a brush of clarity. Julius meant nothing to me other than providing a plug for an emotional gap. Now, here I sit, fleeing him, and a bus-load of people think I'm crazy and dangerous. I know one more thing: if I don't get off this bus now, I will be met by police officers at the next stop. Luckily, we've exited the Turnpike so when I hit the emergency stop, the bus is able to pull over right away.

The doors hiss open and I leap through them as quickly as I can. The bus driver must figure that the safety of his passengers is more important than keeping me contained for the authorities. God bless him.

My duffle bag trailing behind me, I dodge my way along the crowded sidewalk, not allowing myself to stop and think. That way lies nothing but disaster. I continue forward because that is all I know at this point. I have no destination; I have no plan. When I run out of breath, I duck into an alley that empties into a parking lot on the far side of the building. I've slowed down, but I'm still moving. Weaving between cars, I realize my lungs are processing flames rather than air. I need to stop, but I'm still exposed.

Eyeing an oversized SUV, I run for cover, but when I shimmy between the bumpers of two cars, the handle of my duffle bag catches on a trailer hitch. The bag tears open at a seam and my clothes spill to the ground. Stopping here will have to do.

I kneel down and begin stuffing the clothes back into the bag. I pull a belt from the bottom of the pile in order to tie the bag closed when I'm done, but a certain t-shirt catches my eye. It's a green, stretched-out shirt from an agricultural supply company. That in itself is strange, but what's inexplicable is the year printed on the back: 2005.

I glance up from the shirt and am slapped with a vertigo-like feeling as the parking lot dissolves and Aunt Beverly's spare bedroom materializes. I grab the dresser for balance. In my hand is Uncle Clint's green t-shirt that I borrowed earlier this year while doing some chores around the farm. When my head stops spinning, I sit on the floor with my back against the footrest of my bed. I'm shaking uncontrollably, but what's worse is the echoing statement in my head: "Why did you leave me all by myself? Why did you take my son?"

CHAPTER NINETEEN

Once I'm able to get control of myself, I decide to keep it low-key for the rest of the morning. The truth is, I don't think I could handle any interaction with anybody right now. The flashbacks to the times when I was at the peak of my paranoia always take a massive toll on me. My energy is drained and it's all I can do to lift my head up from my pillow. I make the conscious decision to remain prone until lunchtime, but I'm not so sure that I have the ability to choose otherwise.

Aunt Beverly has learned to stop coming to look for me. Uncle Clint, well, he was never really a consideration for seeking me out. The most strenuous activity I perform over the course of the morning is to turn my head to watch the shadow of the house grow shorter on the lawn. Most people would be bored with this, but I utilize a meditation technique I learned when I first moved out here. Unfortunately, while the meditation helped to get my fears and paranoia under control, I believe it also opened up the door to my flashbacks. I've been known to pass hours in a flashback, just as I'm able to pass hours on something as mundane as watching a shadow disappear.

I rise from my waking slumber to eat some of Aunt Beverly's famous pork chops. Uncle Clint is conspicuously absent from the meal, which is an inexcusable trespass at Aunt Beverly's table. I, in turn, shovel the food into my mouth at a pace rapid enough to cause Aunt Beverly to stop and watch me, mouth agape.

Without excuse or explanation, I rise from the table, give her a kiss on the cheek and walk outside, doing everything I can to keep from breaking into a sprint. It's chillier than I had expected, but there's no time to turn back to get a jacket.

I shuffle along the porch, kicking at the small gaps between the boards. Though my head is turned down, my eyes are scanning the area, trying to pick up signs of my uncle. The barn door is swinging in the breeze and I can see the bed of his truck sticking out from behind the tractor. Frankly, I thought the truck would have been gone by the time I got outside. I can see the exhaust spewing from the tailpipe, so at least I know he has the intention of leaving. I think about just asking to tag along, but not only would that not be believable, I don't think I could take another barrage of Hank Williams, Jr. tunes.

I creep around the side of the barn, listening for his voice. When I hear nothing, I continue on to the door, stop, then dash across the opening. Once on the other side, I take a deep breath, preparing myself for my next display of stealth. Slowly, I peer around the corner, pressing my face so hard to the barn that I take a splinter in the cheek. I have to stuff my fist into my mouth to keep from yelping.

Uncle Clint is no more than twenty-five feet away, leaning on the hood of his truck, smoking a stogy. As I watch the ash grow long and the cigar grow short, I realize I have only one option and it's now or never. After plucking the splinter from my face, I shimmy along the ground until I'm just behind the pickup. I get a mouthful of exhaust and almost go reeling into a coughing fit. When that sensation subsides, I lift myself up onto the rear bumper and slip over the tailgate. I slither up until I'm directly behind the rear window so there's no way for him to see me when he looks in his rear-view.

While I wait for him to get in the truck, I come up with a slew of stories to explain what I'm doing here. When the best is, *I thought you might be going to the car wash and figured I needed a shower anyway,* it doesn't take long to realize that if I'm caught I might as well just throw my arms up in surrender like a Frenchman.

Minutes later, Uncle Clint gets into the cab of the truck. I know this not because I hear the door open, but because the truck sinks about a foot and a half. Soon after he slams the door, we're moving. I bounce relentlessly against the sides of the truck bed as we rumble along the dirt path that leads to the main road. The bruises begin to develop along with the idea that maybe this wasn't very intelligent.

We make it out to the asphalt and the ride turns from violent thrashing to calm, even coasting. The slight vibration of the tires rolling over the road is hypnotic. I feel my muscles begin to relax and I turn my gaze skyward, but my body goes rigid when the sky turns from clear azure, filled with the aroma of burning leaves to deep ebony, filled with the putrid stench of diesel exhaust. The air that just a moment ago felt refreshing, is now oppressive.

As the memories of Uncle Clint's truck disappear, I take notice of my surroundings. I lower the tarp that I have pulled up to just below my eyes and peer over the side of the truck bed. Rows of vehicles extend in both directions and a lot full of tractor-trailers lies just beyond. About seventy-five yards away is a squat brick building, low-lit in amber. Brightly lit fast-food and coffee shop signs adorn the entranceway, creating an eerie, yet inviting glow. I could go for both, but if I get up, I risk losing my ride. Besides, who knows what kind of people are in a place like this. I feel fairly secure in this remote area, but my pulse quickens at the thought of going into the building.

I pull the tarp up and settle myself back in among the tools and landscaping equipment with which I'm sharing the truck. There's no sign of life in the parking lot, so it looks like I will be here a little longer. I close my eyes and try to sleep, but I can't stop my mind from wandering to the events of the past few days. The more I try to push those thoughts out of my head, the more my stomach reminds me about just how hungry I am. I haven't had a bite to eat in over twelve hours and that was just half a muffin.

My stomach begins rumbling loud enough that I'm worried it will give me away if the driver returns. I know it's ridiculous, but it's enough to get me to crawl over the far side of the cab and duck between two SUV's. I'm not exactly sure what I've accomplished, but I feel I'm a step closer to acquiring some food.

I try to put everything out of my mind except finding a meal, and this seems to allow me to garner enough courage to stand up and begin the long, lonely trek to *Burger King*. I've taken six consecutive steps when the first person exits the building. Instinctively, I dive out of the aisle, but my aim is unfortunate and I land in a large puddle. Considering I can't remember when it last rained, I pray that it's water.

The sharp sound of dress shoes on concrete changes to the dull sound of dress shoes on asphalt. This person is in no hurry, so I'm stuck in the puddle. With my luck, if I popped up now, they'd think I was attacking them and I'd get a face full of pepper spray or a round-house to the temple.

So I wait patiently.

This occurs two more times before I realize that I'll never be able to eat if I continue on in this manner. Before I rise the final time, I clench my fists, grit my teeth, and tell myself repeatedly that nobody is going to attack me. Nobody is after me. Nobody is going to blow up the rest stop. I stand and walk, all the time repeating these reassurances.

I persevere until I am inside the building. The fluorescent lights are glaring and the noise is deafening. I recoil as if I'd been bombarded with rotten fruit when I crossed the threshold. When I peek out from behind my arm, I see that the deafening noise is erupting from a total of about eight people, none of which, luckily, has seen me come in.

I look from face to face to see if I'm in the company of terrorists, but the crowd looks safe. I've come down a bit from my episode this afternoon, but I'm still edgy. I step over to *Burger King* and wind my way through the snake-like rails even though there's nobody else on line. A young black woman, who is obviously anything but happy to be there, offers an insincere greeting at the register.

As I place my order, I glance over to the *Nathan's* hot dog stand where a man with a dark complexion fiddles with the soda fountain. I try to get a better look without him noticing, but from here it's hard to discern any telltale features. I convince myself that he is Indian, not Middle-Eastern, so I can enjoy my meal, but the uncertainty still tugs at the back of my brain.

Are you going to be fooled that easily? the voice in my head asks. *You're just going to convince yourself that you're not in danger?*

I look around, trying to find something that can distract me from the voice, and spot a television set mounted in the corner of the room. It is tuned to *WABC* out of New York which is airing a special report. It's the first television I've seen in months, and it's not a good sign that there's a special report.

I pay the cashier, pick up the tray of food and move to a table in the center of the room, completely bypassing the condiments and utensils. I'm close enough to the television to hear the report, but far enough away where I'm not really in anybody's direct line of sight.

The program cuts to commercial just as I sit down, so I have to endure this torture for a few more minutes. I try to get a few bites of my food in during the break, but my stomach is practically refusing it. I push a few fries around on the tray and take a sip of my soda. My mind is racing with the possibilities of what could be on that news report. Is it another attack or did the President just have a bout of gas that they need to sensationalize? As much as I'd like to think it's the latter, I'm leaning toward the former.

My survey of the other people in the building is heating up. I've studied the few faces scattered around the tables, the two working the fast food places, and the two behind the *Starbucks* counter. There's also one security guard, but he, like the others, appears harmless. The problem is that appearances can be deceiving. Any one of them could be in bed with the enemy.

A loud buzzing noise seems to suddenly emanate from everywhere. I brace myself, palms down on the table, ready to burst from my seat as soon as I figure out which way is the safest to run. The only thing that keeps me from sprinting at this moment is the fact that nobody else seems to be reacting to the sound.

I take a few deep breaths and look frantically around, trying to find the source of the noise. The news report is back on the television and now I'm frantic to be able to hear it. Then something catches my eye: the neon sign hanging over the condiments table. I fix my concentration on it and do my best to control my breathing. Gradually, the buzzing noise mutes itself.

I release a deep sigh and turn my attention to the small black television set mounted in the corner, but the special report is gone. Immediately, my fears and inhibitions are gone.

"What was it?" I call out.

Everybody looks at me as I stand up and walk toward the television. When nobody answers, I point up at the set and say, "The special report, what was it about?"

Silence.

A woman by the vending machines on the far end of the building tiptoes out through doors. I don't try to stop her. I'm not here to hurt anyone or scare anybody; I just want to know what the news report is about. Unfortunately, I've forgotten that I've been riding in the back of a landscaper's truck for an hour. My clothes are a bit rumpled and dirty. My hair's a mess. I've probably got grease smeared on my face.

But none of that matters. Why shouldn't these people answer a simple question? Unless they're hiding something.

I turn to the man nearest me and do my best to speak in a quiet, rational voice.

"Please," I beg, "what happened?"

"It was just a story about some guy they took into custody in New York. Somebody that was responsible for something that happened this morning."

But I'm not listening. The guard is making his way toward me, a menacing look plastered on his face. He's a good fifty pounds overweight and probably just as many years past his prime, but I don't feel like having any type of confrontation.

"Custody," I mumble to the man who answered my question, the whole time watching the guard.

"Yeah. He killed some Arab this morning. Claims the guy was a terrorist, but nobody else seems to see it that way."

This grabs my attention, but the guard is on me. He grabs my arm firmly and "suggests" that I leave. I shake free of him and ask the man to continue with his explanation. The guard lets out a huff, so I beg him to give me just one minute.

"How did they catch him?" I ask.

"His buddies turned him in. Good thing, too. There was no surveillance video of the attack."

"His buddies?"

"Yeah. I guess he asked them to help him follow the dead guy's buddy, so that he could kill him off, too. They didn't want any part of it, so they tipped the police off. They remained anonymous, though, so the police were forced to use the Arab guy as bait to catch the murderer."

I think about how close I was to being in that car when the police closed in. I could be sitting in prison right now, if I hadn't finally gotten brave enough to put my foot down.

The guard nods at me. "I think you've got everything you want. Why don't you take off? You've scared enough people around here tonight."

I don't argue. I just hope I can get my feet to carry me where I need to go. Leaving my food behind, I run out through the door, figuring I might as well build up momentum so that when the fear sets in, I'll be farther along than if I'd been walking.

The cold night air slaps me as I break through the exterior doors, but it's invigorating and gives me enough energy to make it all the way to the line of tractor-trailers. When I get there, a very American-looking young man wearing jeans, a trucking company jacket, and a baseball cap is about to enter the cab of his truck.

"Any chance I can catch a ride?" I ask, trying to appear calm and collected. I'm probably filthy, but hopefully he'll look past that.

He looks me up and down. "Where are you headed?"

"Anywhere. Just not here."

"Trouble? I don't want trouble."

"No. No trouble. I'm not running from anything but bad memories."

He considers this for a minute and then nods his head. "Okay, hop in."

CHAPTER TWENTY

I manage to keep out of sight for the entire ride, even when I snap out of my flashback and was startled to find myself in Uncle Clint's truck. The ride isn't long and, to be honest, Uncle Clint isn't that observant, so I probably could have sat up in the back without him noticing. He parks in a small lot in town that serves a strip of shops. I wait, trying desperately to figure out just when would be the perfect time to hop out: before he gets out or after? Either way, if I'm not careful I have a good chance of being spotted.

The brief wait becomes an unbearable one, so I try to poke my head up to window level in order to catch a glimpse of what he's doing. He's got his cell phone out, but I don't get to observe much else since I'm forced to duck again when he lifts his gaze to the rear-view mirror. That makes up my mind. I have to get out now before he discovers my scraggly ass.

Slowly, so as not to make a sound, I push myself into the front passenger-side corner of the truck bed. I wait in silence to see if I've been discovered and when I feel confident that I have not, I roll over the side, keeping my body pressed to the truck. I remind myself of the old Christmas cartoon where the Grinch slinks his way through Whoville on his fat little belly.

I try to remain focused on my uncle, knowing that even the slightest thing can send me reeling into a flashback. If I was ever going to get control of these things it needs to be now. The last thing I can afford is to zone out for a while, only to find out when I come out of it that Uncle Clint has already returned home and I'm stuck in town.

Lucky for me, his passenger-side mirror has been missing for over a year. Well, actually it's not so much luck as it is the fact that I side-swiped the barn last year trying to help out a little bit around the farm. Either way, it works in my favor now as I press my ear to the passenger door in an attempt to hear Uncle Clint's conversation.

I catch the phrases, "I'm here" and "I'll let you know how it goes" before he hangs up and gets out of the truck. As he walks down the aisle, I slink along between the cars. Eventually, he waddles his way into a travel agency. I saunter across the street and take a seat at a table on the sidewalk outside a coffee shop. When the waiter arrives, I ask him to bring me a large cappuccino and a newspaper. Within minutes, I'm peering at the travel agency over the top of the sports section of the *Colorado Springs Gazette*.

Through the window, I can see the back of my uncle's head. I can't gain a heck of a lot of information from here, but at least I can keep track of him. I start working my Hardy Boys magic and try to deduce why my uncle would be in a travel agency. Only two things come to mind: either he is very serious with this other woman and he plans on traveling to meet her or I *have* been overreacting and he's planning a trip for him and Aunt Beverly. I'd like to believe the latter, but I know that neither of them have ever been on a plane or really traveled very far outside the great state of Colorado for that matter. It doesn't mean people can't change, but I know my aunt would never fly, so what kind of trip would he need a travel agency for?

I sip my cappuccino and turn the page of the newspaper, just in case anybody is watching me. When I'm done, I decide I won't be able to find out much more from here so I pay for the drink and head back to the truck. I get myself settled back into the bed and hope that my uncle

remains as clueless as usual. Another ten minutes later, he lives up to
my expectations and we are on the road again, just me, Uncle Clint,
and Hank Williams, Jr.

As the rumble of the road begins to take over once again, I mull over
what I've discovered: secret phone calls almost constantly and a meeting with a travel agent. Okay, so maybe I'm not the best detective in
the world, but it's a start. I'm a little hesitant though, because if he *is*
planning a surprise trip for Aunt Beverly, when I tell her what's been
going on, it will ruin the surprise.

I'll have to wrestle with this one for a while. We hit the highway and
the smooth vibration begins to once again send me into a daze. The
world goes out of focus for a moment and when it comes back I'm in
the cab of a tractor-trailer. I sit up straight and rub my eyes. I blink
hard a few times, stalling in order to figure out just where I am. After a
few acrobatic stretches, I scoop the crud out of the corner of my eyes.
Nope, still no idea where I am.

"Morning," says the driver. "You must have been exhausted. You
were out not five minutes after we left the rest stop."

"Oh, right," I reply as the events of the previous night begin to
come into focus. "How long have I been asleep?"

"About eight hours. You didn't even wake up when we stopped for
fuel and coffee. I didn't want to disturb you, but there's a bacon and
egg sandwich in that bag there. Cup of coffee is in the cup holder."

"Thanks," I mutter as I tear open the brown paper bag. The sandwich is gone before I even take my first sip of coffee. Maybe even
before I breathe. "Where are we?"

"Approaching Pittsburgh."

"Really?" I ask, looking out at the vast expanse of fields and mountains. "Doesn't seem like we're heading into a city."

"It's a small city. When we get closer you'll start to see some of the
big buildings and bridges."

Big buildings and bridges. Targets. Any of these fields outside could be the one that Flight 93 crashed into. I glance to the sky to make sure that nothing is falling from it.

As if on cue, the driver says, "You should have seen it a couple of miles back. There was a sign advertising tours of the site where Flight 93 crashed. You believe that shit? People will try to make a buck off anything."

I nod. This is all bad.

"It's like those people who have been scamming the insurance companies and all that. Claiming they lost people in the attacks and collecting money. What's with that? Is nothing sacred anymore?"

"Can we talk about something else?" I ask, sounding a bit more pleading than I would have liked.

He glances over at me and I can almost feel him trying to read my face. "Ok, sure."

"How far out of the city are we?" I ask, as the fields begin to give way to more industrial looking buildings. Truck stops and fast food restaurant signs begin to populate the landscape.

"Technically, we're there. Outlying suburbs, really, but for all intents and purposes, this is Pittsburgh."

In the distance I can see the downtown skyline begin to come into view. For the first time it hits me that I am about to enter a city. I can't go there. Who knows what will happen. Terrorists are plotting to hit us in new places every day. No, I need to get out now.

"Can you drop me off?" I ask. The panic in my voice is hardly disguised.

"Where?"

"Anywhere. Just somewhere before we get into the city."

"There's not really anywhere to …"

"Please!"

"Yeah, ok," he says, with a tone that adds, *the sooner the better.*

Just past the next exit, he pulls the rig off to the shoulder of the road. The truck has barely come to a complete stop when he looks over at me.

"Getting off and back onto the highway is a pain in the ass. Mind getting out here?"

I look outside at the cars whizzing by at seventy and eighty miles per hour. On the other side of us the exit ramp leads down to a toll booth and through a strip of motels and fast food restaurants. I grab the cup of coffee and open the door.

"Thanks," I say.

"Don't worry about it. I was heading this way anyway."

"No, not for the ride. For not asking too many questions. I appreciate it."

He nods. "It doesn't take long in this job to learn to mind your own business. It's safer for everybody."

I nod and thank him again as I climb down from the cab. I've barely stepped clear of the rig before he pulls away. After coughing out the cloud of diesel exhaust I managed to inhale, I hop the guard rail and scamper down the hill that forms the exit ramp. To my right: a busy street, never-ending traffic, motels, restaurants, stores. To my left: a grassy hill hidden under the exit ramp. The choice is easy.

I toss my duffle bag into the grass and lay down on the ground. If I can figure out my next move, I'll feel more comfortable. I just wish I had somebody to share some of this with—somebody who could help me out, point me in the right direction, but once again, I'm alone.

I could head up the road, get a room, get a hot meal, and think rationally about my situation, but just the thought of the number of cars and people down there and how many of them might be terrorists smuggling dirty bombs into the city sends a shiver through my entire body. Any one of those trucks could be the one that goes boom. Hell, the one that brought me here could be the one. My God, I might have been that close. Was that driver a terrorist? No, no way. But he *was* in quite a hurry to get to the city, right? He couldn't even be bothered to get off the highway to drop me off. Damn it. Did I let him slip through my fingers?

I clutch my bag to my chest, hoping it will protect me from any danger that might come my way. My big, bad duffle bag. Protector of all that is good. It could stop a bullet, right? A nuclear explosion?

Suddenly, the base of this slope seems extremely exposed. I scuttle up the hill and press my back to the concrete support where I can see just about every angle from which somebody would be able to approach me. A gusty wind is blowing, causing the long grass to lie down flat. I turn my back to the wind to avoid breathing in the grit it's blowing around. That's when I hear him and I know that this stay is short-lived.

"Hey, what are you doing back there?" he calls.

My fight-or-flight reaction kicks in and I'm on my feet, ready to do whatever is necessary to survive (which is usually the 'flight' option). The odd thing is, when I spring to my feet there is a hollow metallic sound, nothing like what would be made by a dirt and grass hill. No, the sound is more like the noise you'd hear if you were to jump to your feet in, say, the bed of a pickup truck.

Before I even bother to look around, I know that the hill, the exit ramp, and all of Pittsburgh are long gone. Unfortunately, I need to come up with a quick explanation for Uncle Clint about why I am in the back of his truck.

"I asked ya a question, boy? What are you doin' back there?"

His face is cherry red and sweat is running in streams from his forehead. Anger or nerves? At the moment, it doesn't matter. Come on, Jim, think of something. How could you not be prepared with a story? Think. Come on, you can come up with something.

"You been spyin' on me?" he bellows.

Well, so much for needing to come up with a story. I mean, he's not all that bright, but I don't think he's really very gullible either. *I fell asleep*, probably wouldn't get me very far.

"No," is all I can muster.

"The hell you ain't."

"I ain't ... wasn't."

"Git your sorry ass outta my truck."

I hop out. No sense in arguing that. We end up standing face to face and I do my best to act like I'm not intimidated.

"You mind tellin' me now just what you're doin' back there?" he growls.

I turn my options over in my head, but quickly realize the truth is the only thing that will even make sense. I guess that's my only play.

"Tailing you," I reply.

"Tailing me? So, you were spying."

"I'm on to you, Uncle Clint. I know what you're up to. Travel plans? Who are you going to visit?"

"Just what are you accusin' me of?"

"Oh, nothing," I coo. My mocking tone incenses him. He grabs my shirt in both hands and slams my body into his truck. His face is an inch from mine and I can feel his hot breath on me. Even though I'm still resolved to complete my mission, I'm a little embarrassed about being caught. I turn my head and avert my eyes so as not to see the elemental ire in his.

"Look at me," he growls. "Be a man and look at me."

I turn my head back to face him, but my eyes remain averted. His breath is smoky and stale, and he uses it like a weapon. I cringe away and wish I could crawl under the truck.

"Let go of me," I whimper.

Way to go, Jim. Manly.

"So, what, ya think ya got it all figured out?"

"I have you figured out, yeah."

"Tell me then what ya got in your head there?"

"You're running around on Aunt Beverly! It's obvious. You couldn't be *more* obvious. Secret phone calls, secret trips to the travel agent. We both know Aunt Beverly doesn't fly."

He shakes his head and lets go of me with one final shove. He looks like he's about to say something, maybe even something profound, then he dismisses me with a huff and a wave of his hand.

I get my balance, smooth my shirt and try to exude some sense of dignity. I don't know to who I'm trying to portray this, but I try anyway. I take a deep breath and realize my hands are shaking. I want to take the time to calm myself down completely, but I realize that I need to get to Aunt Beverly before he does, before he fills her mind with lies. I need to tell her everything now.

CHAPTER TWENTY-ONE

Aunt Beverly sits vulnerable on that completely uncomfortable mahogany Victorian chair reading a Mary Higgins Clark mystery. Her back is straight and her feet rest side by side, flat on the floor. A cup of tea sits on the small table at her side, steam still rising from the surface.

I almost hate to ruin her perfect little fantasy world—the one in which Uncle Clint is a faithful husband—but I've been left no choice but to make a pre-emptive strike. As I walk into the room, I mull over the myriad ways I can broach the subject. Not a single one of them is good.

Five minutes after I enter the room she still has not acknowledged my presence. Either it's a good book or I'm invisible. Not knowing much about the works of Mary Higgins Clark, I check my hands to rule out the latter. Still there. So I'm not invisible, that's good.

I clear my throat.

"I know you're there, Jim," she says without taking her eyes from the page. "I'm just trying to finish this chapter."

"I can wait," I tell her, nervously glancing down the hallway to see if Uncle Clint is coming. Nope. So far, so good. I lean back and rest my right hand on the wooden arm of the sofa. As I look around the room, trying to find something to capture my interest, I tap my fingernails in succession, repeatedly.

Ba-da-da-dum.

Ba-da-da-dum.

Ba-da-da-dum.

The mystery novel is slammed shut and Aunt Beverly sighs. She removes her reading glasses and rubs the bridge of her nose, then takes a sip of her tea.

"Finished?" I ask.

She glares at me.

"I can come back if I've caught you at a bad time," I offer, knowing I need to address this now, but still looking for any reason to chicken out.

"What is it, Jim?" she asks. There is little humor in her voice, or curiosity for that matter.

"That tea looks good. Is there any more? I can boil some more water."

"James, if you don't tell me what you want, I'm going to boil you. Now what is it?"

I purse my lips and decide that short, sweet, and to the point is the approach I need to take. I take a deep breath before spilling everything I know.

"Uncle Clint is having an affair," I say. I try to prepare for her response, but I have no idea how she is going to react. Scream? Cry? Laugh? She can go any way with this.

She studies me for at least two full minutes, which makes me feel uncomfortable. I spent a couple of years with people looking at me funny and this reminds me of all that a bit too much. I give her another moment to absorb what I told her.

"An affair?"

I nod.

She nods.

I crease my brow.

She creases hers.

I can't tell if we're contemplating what I told her or playing a game of monkey-see, monkey-do. After a minute, she puts her reading glasses back on and opens her book.

"Aunt Beverly?"

"Yes?"

"Did you understand what I told you?"

"I'm old, Jim, not stupid."

"I didn't say ..."

"However, if you believe what you just told me, then I'm afraid you're young *and* stupid."

I sit back on the sofa, deflated. How could she not believe me? I mean, sure, I've been paranoid and depressed for the past few years. Sure, I've made huge issues out of nothing. Sure, my crazy conspiracy theories have alienated me from my family and friends. But this is different!

"I ..."

"Not another word," she says. "Now, I'm going to read my book. I'd appreciate it if you'd give me some peace and quiet."

I stand up, a million different things dancing around my tongue, ready to explode out through my lips, but I keep it all in. Maybe she's right. If she's so convinced, why shouldn't I be? She didn't even ask me what proof I had, which is probably a good thing since there's not much I could have given her.

Though, if I could just get that proof then she'd believe me. If that's what it takes, then that's what I'll get. I veer off toward the kitchen so I can see if Uncle Clint is out back. I don't know how I'm going to get evidence, but something will come to me. I stop just inside the back door and look at the phone mounted on the wall. Could it be this simple? Is there any chance he would have been stupid enough to call and leave his mistress' number on redial?

I pick the receiver up off the cradle and place it to my ear, but I flinch when it turns out to be colder than I expected. I pull the phone away and notice that it has turned from a pleasant yellow to the foreboding black of one of the country's fast-disappearing pay phones.

The phone, of course, isn't the only thing that's changed. Everything around me has changed. The farmhouse? Gone. Uncle Clint? Gone. Aunt Beverly? Well, she's kind of gone. Everything but her voice.

"Hello?" I squeak, in a weak, quivering voice. "Aunt Bev?"

"James, is that you? Oh my Lord, I've been so worried about you. Jimmy, where are you?"

I look around and it takes a few minutes before I remember that I'm outside Pittsburgh. The sites are so alien to me, yet the feel of a city pervades my entire being.

"Pittsburgh. Some town just outside. Something like that. I think I remember a sign saying New Kensington."

As I explain this to her, I gradually speed up, as if the urgency to tell her everything is increasing by the second. In the back of my mind, though, something tickles my thoughts. I do have to tell her everything, yet no matter how much I babble on, nothing seems to be the *right* thing.

"Jim, slow down," she says. "Is there somewhere nearby, a landmark or something? A gas station where you can ask for information?"

I glance up and down the street which seems to have about fifteen gas stations.

"Yeah, yeah. They're here, but …"

"But what?"

"I can't go to them. I'm afraid. I'm too afraid to move, but I'm too afraid to stay here."

"Okay, Jim, honey, just calm down. We're going to get you."

She continues talking. Something about calling the police, but I'm not listening. What is it that I wanted to tell her? I look at the phone in my hand and the *right* thought seems to push itself forward, but there is a strong membrane that it can't seem to penetrate. It is extremely frustrating.

"Okay, Jim? Are you listening?"

"No, I'm sorry Aunt Bev. I wasn't."

"The police, Jim. Call them. Have them pick you up. Then we'll come out and get you, but it could take a long time for your uncle to get there."

"I can't go to the police. They'll lock me up."

There is a hesitation, then she asks, "Jim, have you done something wrong?"

I can feel the pain in her voice, the anguish in the question. Images of Julius and a dead Middle-Eastern man flash through my mind, but then, and I can't for the life of me figure out why, an image of Uncle Clint comes to mind. He's pushing me up against his truck, yelling at me. It's so vivid, but the strangest part is I think Uncle Clint drives a station wagon.

Finally, I manage to answer her. "No. I'm just afraid they might think I'm …"

I can't say it. *Crazy.* There, I can think it. I just can't say it. I can hear her holding back sobs on the other end. What am I doing to that poor woman? I shouldn't have called.

"Jimmy, you listen to me and listen to me good. Do you see a motel?"

I looked down the street.

No, that's not right.

I *look* down the street. Right?

Okay, I look down the street and see a motel.

"Yes."

"Go there. I don't want to hear any ands, ifs, or buts about it. Just go. When you get there, get a room and call me from there. I will send Uncle Clint immediately. Luckily, he finally bought a new truck with some of that money your mother left us. The old wagon would have never made the trip."

I slink to the ground, keeping the earpiece to my ear. The mouthpiece was up in the air—no, the mouthpiece *is* up in the air—away from my mouth. I told her I would try. Why does that keep happening? Did this already occur somewhere in my past? Why does none of this feel right?

I hang up the phone and walk slowly across the street, forcing one foot out in front of the other. It's twenty minutes before I'm across to the other sidewalk. Aunt Beverly must be sick to her stomach. Uncle Clint, though, is probably off with some floozy. I recoil at the inappropriateness of this thought. My uncle and I have never really gotten along, but that was a pretty harsh thought, regardless. The idea, though, sparks something in my brain and I suddenly feel like I'm in a house somewhere holding a yellow phone, but that image quickly fades away.

Whatever semblance of sanity I had left is, without a doubt, gone. I can't even keep my life straight. My timeline seems to be fading in and out, but for some reason this, my reality, seems false. I make it into the motel lobby and manage to rent a room, despite how I must look. Well, I'm sure it didn't hurt that I was able to pay in advance with cash.

A few minutes later, I'm in my room dialing Aunt Beverly's phone number. It rings once, twice, but while it does, the house comes back again. The phone turns from the boring beige of a motel phone to the refreshing yellow of Aunt Beverly's kitchen decorations. A moment later, the call is answered. This time I don't slip back into the past.

"Nettles' Feed and Grain," the voice says. I place the phone on the hook. I guess the last call Uncle Clint made wasn't to the mystery woman, at least not from this phone. My first lead is a dead end.

I sit down on the floor beneath the phone and place my head in my hands, trying to steady the waves of pressure that seem to be oscillating from one side to the other. I have a feeling I won't be chasing after Uncle Clint for a little while.

Chapter Twenty-two

Four Rolaids, two Advil, and a forty-five minute nap later, I'm beginning to feel normal, though slightly groggy. That last flashback kicked my ass. I've never had a reaction like this before, but then again I've never become aware of my situation while in the middle of one of the episodes. Despite the fact that my mind feels like it was tied up inside a sack before being indiscriminately kicked and beaten by a rogue gang of mind-hating ogres, this new development is encouraging, as so few things are these days.

The sun has already begun its descent into the mountain peaks to the west. There were days when I was so angry with the world that if I could manage to watch the sunset, I would do so in hopes that the sun would simply impale itself on the highest apex, bleeding out its light, never to shine its warmth on the world again. Of course I knew that wasn't possible, but a guy can hope, can't he?

Now, though, things are different. I've got a mission (one from which I was briefly distracted, granted, but a mission nonetheless). And it's not a simple task to accomplish. That Uncle Clint, he's a wily ol' bastard. I'm going to have to be awfully clever to catch him.

I contemplate my next step over a good shave. It's been a few days, so the beard is thick. It feels good to rid my face of the bristly creature that all too often takes up residence there. When it's gone, I splash on some of my uncle's Old Spice aftershave, then bask in the tingling sensation as the alcohol finds its way into my open pores.

The entire time I'm shaving, my mind is at work trying to figure out the best way to incriminate Uncle Clint. Photographs and videotape are always good options, but I'm no Cecil B. DeMille (fine, I have no idea who he is, but I'm pretty sure he made movies). Also, there's the serious lack of recording equipment to consider. That would definitely hinder my ability to capture Uncle Clint's exploits on tape.

There's the possibility of hiring a private detective, but I currently don't have ready access to my inheritance. Aunt Beverly wisely invested it for me. Lack of anything resembling a job finishes ruling out that course of action, but the idea itself brings back anxiety about the private detective that is waiting to speak to me. Maybe I can promise to speak to him in exchange for some investigative work. It seems promising, but I'm still not convinced I can talk to him. Opening myself up to that part of my past could be torture.

Hey, torture is an option. I spend a lot of time thinking about this idea, mostly because I know I could never do it. I'm too squeamish. I don't even like to kill spiders. I leave that task up to my aunt. Anyway, I realize after a while that in most of my torture fantasies I never even bother to get any evidence, I just keep torturing and torturing and torturing, which isn't exactly the point of all this. Oh well, I wasn't going to do that one anyway.

Occasionally, Doubt creeps up behind me, taps me on the shoulder and runs away. It does this repeatedly. It does it enough to distract me and make me wander from my course. Before I know it, I'm swinging my arms wildly around, trying to smack Doubt in the head. All the time, the little bastard is giggling at me, diving through my legs, hiding behind chairs, and downright just pissing me off.

The truth is that Aunt Beverly's reaction was anything but one of concern. She was in complete denial. Maybe I should follow her lead and let it roll off my shoulders, or maybe she actually knows what's going on and doesn't care. That thought stupefies me. How could that be?

Eventually, I grab the little imp called Doubt by the collar and beat him into submission. Quitting is not an option. I have to think, damn it. I need to be clever.

Frustrated, I go to my room and grab one of my many flannel shirts from the closet. Slinging it over my shoulder, I walk back out to the family room. The television set is dark as it almost always seems to be when the sun's up, unless I'm seated in front of it. I throw myself onto the couch because lying prone and staring at the ceiling will obviously solve all my problems.

It's only a second or two before I notice something small and cold digging into the back of my neck, so I reach behind my head and grab a handful of whatever it is before yanking it out. It turns out to be a zipper. The zipper belongs to a coat. The coat belongs to my wonderful uncle.

Before I can discard it like a pair of soiled underwear, something in the pocket catches my eye. I sit up, check to make sure nobody is going to walk in on me, then remove the object from the coat pocket.

It's a note he must have jotted down at the travel agency.

I scan down the sheet of paper and notice three letters in particular: SFO. I believe that's the San Francisco airport. Arriving? Tomorrow! That son-of-a-bitch has the gall to fly his little trollop here.

At least he's making my job easy. All I have to do is be there. I can get a camera for this. I won't need a zoom lens or any fancy infra-red crap. In a crowded airport I'll be able to get a picture of them from ten feet away before they even notice I'm there. This is perfect. In a crowded airport, I'll be … well, I'll be in a crowded airport. For a moment, my mind is made up to drop the whole thing, but I know Aunt Beverly needs my help. Somehow, I'm going to have to force myself to do this. Somehow, I, who can barely imagine an airport without total mental collapse, will have to walk right into the middle of a real one. Okay. I can do this. I don't know how, but I know I can.

Taking a deep breath, I spring from the sofa with renewed energy, but quickly sit down again as the world goes dark and I narrowly escape passing out from a head rush. I give myself a moment to recover and the world begins to come back into focus. Staying here for a few minutes might be a good thing. Besides, what am I going to do now? Not much can happen until tomorrow.

I look into the dark television screen and study the distorted reflection there. It's mostly a silhouette of me and some furniture against the fading light permeating the Venetian blinds. I trace my outline with my eyes, but when I shift to the contours of the furniture, the lines strike me as odd. I turn away from the television set and Aunt Beverly's furniture has become that of a run down motel.

There is no time to prepare myself. Immediately, I'm back in that motel outside Pittsburgh, waiting for my uncle to arrive. This place is much dingier than the one in Fort Lee. It appears that the curtains and the décor haven't been changed since the seventies and, apparently, either have the sheets on the bed. I sit on the edge of the mattress, not wanting to touch anything. The television is off because I'm too scared to look at the outside world, yet I'm really not all that fond of this inside world.

Hours pass with no contact with another human being. After my initial call to my aunt, I told her I'd feel better not using the phone. I don't know if that was a mistake or not, but it's a decision I've stuck with.

Time continued ... continues ... to pass, as it always does, but I have no idea how much of it is actually slipping past me. I have a vague awareness of the objects in the room becoming enveloped in darkness only to return with the light of morning, but when all of that actually happened or *if* all of that actually happened, I have no clue.

I stare into the television set and feel as if it could transport me to a whole new place and time. I have some kind of ridiculous feeling that if I concentrate hard enough, I can teleport myself to Aunt Beverly's house. For a lack of anything better to do, I try. I concentrate so hard I almost pass out, but something happens. The room fades, only to be replaced by what seems to be Aunt Beverly's family room. I can make out the television and sofa and floor lamp. I can see the detail in her wallpaper, though it is a little dark in the room. I can even smell something cooking, but as quickly as it all appeared, it is gone.

My head throbs as what remains of my sanity tries to convince the rest of my brain that what I thought I just saw could not possibly have been real, but my brain does not want to let go. Suddenly, the rest of my brain goes on the offensive and attempts to convince the "sane" part that what *it* thinks is real is nothing but a false reality. I latch on to this assault and find myself ringing in with a chorus of "Yeah!"s and "You tell 'em!"s. Though I'm verbalizing encouragement to my own brain in an imaginary fight it's having with another part of itself, it feels right.

The more I fight, the fuzzier the motel room becomes. I start to think of everything as if it happened before. I am no longer sitting in a motel room. I *was* sitting in a motel room. I'm not waiting for Uncle Clint. I *waited* for Uncle Clint. Nothing seemed real or tangible anymore. Nothing.

Except the knock on the door.

When I heard it, I fought with every last ounce of willpower I had, but it was no use. With what felt like the most intense head rush in the history of mankind, I am sucked back into that motel outside of Pittsburgh. I try for a moment to build up that concentration again, but the knock continues and I soon forget that I had done anything other than wait in silence for my uncle.

I creep up to the door, trying not to let anyone on the other side know I'm responding, just in case my visitors aren't friendly. I try to look through the peephole from as far back as possible, so that whoever is on the other side doesn't notice a change of light. Through the lens I see a heavy, but sturdy looking man. His expression is serious, but extremely familiar. Uncle Clint has arrived.

Before I can open the door, a vision of a piece of paper flashes before my eyes. It's too quick a thought for me to register it as it's happening, but the after-image it leaves burnt into my brain tells me it was a handwritten note with the letters SFO on it. I have no idea what was on the rest of the note or what it has to do with anything that is happening, so I ignore it.

I press my eye to the peephole, to ensure that my mind wasn't playing tricks on me, but also to get a look at more of the hallway so I can guarantee that Uncle Clint isn't knocking on the door under duress. I see no shadows or movement, so I slowly begin to unlatch the door while I continue to watch. My uncle appears agitated so I stop. Am I absolutely positive that nobody is out there with him?

He looks down the hallway then back at the door. It isn't until he rolls his eyes and hollers at me to get a move on that I realize his impatience is because of me, not some mysterious third-party. I open the door, grab him by the shoulder and usher him into the room. A quick glance down the hall in each direction and the door is closed and locked behind him.

Uncle Clint gets a look at me for the first time and I can see the shock in his eyes. He doesn't say a word at first. I don't blame him. I probably look like hell.

"Boy, what in creation happened to you?" he finally asks.

Nice to see you, too.

"A lot," I reply. "Too much."

He studies me and dismisses me with a shake of his head.

"It's not just me," I continue, "it's everyone. You, Aunt Beverly, the motel manager, it doesn't matter. If you survived 9/11, then you're just like me. They're everywhere, these terrorists. Everywhere. It's just that most people don't realize the false security we're living under. They're watching us, waiting, determining our weaknesses and finding ways to exploit them. They want more death and destruction. They want pain. And not just for men, but pain for our women and children. They are beasts. Minions of Satan himself and they will not stop until every last one of us suffers."

"Yup. Okay, get your bags, we've got a long ride."

I stare at him, dumbfounded. "Didn't you hear a word I said?"

"Every last one. Don't know what half of 'em mean and don't care. I'm here to pick you up and bring you home, not to assist you in your trip to the loony bin."

Dejected, I mope my way over to my bag, mope it up off the floor, mope into the bathroom where I mope out a piss I apparently neglected to take in the last twelve hours, then mope to the door. "Let's go," I mope.

He opens the door and leads me down the hallway and out into the parking lot. There are a few times where it takes a physical effort on his part to keep me moving, but eventually my torn bag and I are loaded up into his nice, new truck waiting to leave. He hops into the driver's side, instructs me to buckle my seatbelt, and pulls the truck away from the curb. We are on our way.

When we're out on the highway, he grabs a paper bag from the floor and thrusts it at me. When I open it, the sweet aroma of chicken and dumplings wafts out at me, which is strange because the bag contains a McDonald's cheeseburger and fries.

"Dinner's ready," he says. I stare at him in wonder because I've never heard Uncle Clint do an impersonation of Aunt Beverly before and it was spot-on. When he continues to do it, I realize that something is not right because his lips aren't moving and he's not even looking in my direction.

Suddenly, I remember my little episode in the motel room. I close my eyes and concentrate. When I re-open them, I'm looking at the warm, kind face of my aunt.

"Sorry, what did you say?" I ask, knowing I missed something.

"I asked why you're always sitting in the dark."

"Oh," I mutter, as I realize that the sun has now completely set. "I was thinking about taking a nap. Didn't know dinner would be ready so soon." It's a lie, but a harmless one.

"Well it is, so get washed up and come on inside before it gets cold. We're having chicken and dumplings."

"I know," I say, my mind still contemplating my ride back from Pittsburgh. "It smells wonderful."

CHAPTER
TWENTY-THREE

The day's developments, though dizzying, are comforting, which allows for one of the best nights of sleep I've had since before the 9/11 attacks. I wake to a crisp autumn day with a cloudless sky. The aroma of burning wood pervades the room, indicating that Uncle Clint has decided to light the first fire of the season. Aunt Beverly loves to have a fire burning in the fireplace from the moment the temperature drops below fifty until, oh, the end of April or so.

Uncle Clint's lover isn't arriving from San Francisco until late afternoon so I just have to sit around and wait until …

Okay, snag in the plans. How the hell am I supposed to get to the airport? *Hey, Uncle Clint, can I hitch a ride with you to the airport so I can snap a few photographs of you cheating on your wife of forty years?* probably isn't going to work. No car, no money. Time to be clever again.

I go out to the kitchen where Aunt Beverly is sipping at a hot cup of tea and reading the newspaper. She looks up at me and gives a gentle smile that makes her eyes sparkle. It's the same smile my mother used to give me when I'd finally wake up on a Saturday morning.

"Aunt Bev?"

"Yes?" She folds her paper and places it down on the table. I guess after yesterday's encounter she figures all resistance is futile.

"Can I get a little bit of my money?"

"How much is a little bit?" She rises from the table and goes to the stove where she pours herself another cup of tea.

"I don't know. A hundred?"

"Jim, what on earth do you need a hundred dollars for? I feed you, I give you shelter, and you never leave the house." She sits back down and waits for my answer.

For once, couldn't things just be simple? I just want to help her and I get the Inquisition.

"There's a gift I want to buy. Can we leave it at that, please?"

She gets up with a huff and disappears to her bedroom. When she returns, she's got a handful of twenties. She hands them to me with such apprehension you'd think she was handing over her famous secret funnel cake recipe.

"Thank you," I call back over my shoulder after snatching the money from her and running out the door. Score one for Jimbo.

Stopping in the yard to count the cash (there's an extra twenty in the bundle and I'm sure it didn't find its way in there by accident), I contemplate my next move. Though $120 is enough to get me back and forth to Colorado Springs by bus, I still have a slight aversion to public transportation. That means trains and taxis are out of consideration, too. Spying on Uncle Clint by hiding in the back of his truck is probably only a one-time success, no matter how thick-headed he may be, so it looks like I will have to calm my already racing heart and hop on a bus.

Of course, there's always the issue of the blackouts. Something like a bus ride could easily trigger a flashback. I don't know if I can take that risk. What if I have one that keeps me from getting to the airport in time? What if I miss getting off the bus?

As I stand in the middle of the driveway contemplating my options, a rumble begins to grow in the distance and a cloud of dust rises back

among the trees. The sound grows louder until a Jeep Cherokee rounds
the bend and pulls up alongside the barn.

My answer may have just driven up. A moment later, he steps out of
the car, waving to Uncle Clint who has just emerged from the barn.

"Hello, Clinton," he calls.

"Ray," Uncle Clint acknowledges. "Dresser done?"

"Got her right here," Mr. Peterson replies, patting the Jeep. Uncle
Clint nods and disappears again without so much as an offer of assis-
tance.

I watch impatiently as Ray Peterson goes to the back of his truck
and begins to struggle with the dresser that he refinished for Aunt Beverly.

"Hi, Mr. Peterson," I say, as I position myself on the other side of
the dresser. I think his Jeep just became my transportation into the
city. We wiggle the piece of furniture, trying to get the corners out
from a spot that should have been physically impossible for them to
squeeze into in the first place.

"I knew I shoulda thrown it in the pickup," he laments.

"How'd you get it in here?" I grunt as I strain against the bumper
for leverage.

"Same way we're takin' it out."

"Im … poss … i … ble," I pant.

I'm almost horizontal now, with both feet pressed to the bumper.
Finally, the dresser gives, and I'm lucky Mr. Peterson is there to keep it
from coming down on top of me as I crash to the dirt.

He looks at me sitting on the ground and an expression of exhaustion gradually becomes one of bewilderment before fading into a smile
that grows to full-blown laughter. I allow myself a small laugh and it
feels great. After a few moments, I regain my dignity, grab one side of
the dresser and help him carry it to the house.

"Anything on that detective?" he asks as we walk up to the house.

I nod. "There was a showdown here the other day. Uncle Clint
almost shot him." I let out a small laugh to let him know I'm not seri-

ous, but he knows Uncle Clint well enough to believe that he would have shot somebody for trespassing.

"It turned out all right, though."

"Good," he groans as he heaves the dresser up to get a better grip.

"Hey, Mr. Peterson, can I ask you a favor?"

"Sure," he replies, backing slowly onto the steps. "What is it?"

"Do you have some time today? I need to get to the airport to meet somebody. It's a surprise for my aunt and uncle so I can't really ask them."

"Well that sounds nice. There's no bus?"

He doesn't know about my issues. Nobody really does. Aunt Beverly always made it clear that my paranoia was nobody's business but our own.

"Just charters, I think. Besides, I'm not real good with buses," I reply, hoping it's enough.

He stops to rest the dresser on his knee, looks up at the sky as if the answer to my request is written up there. Either that or maybe he's asking God to spare him a heart attack until we get the dresser inside. Whichever it is, he shrugs.

"You need a ride back?" he asks, before committing.

"Nah, just a ride there. There'll be plenty of taxis to take back, but we'll need to leave right after we put this down, if that's okay."

I don't want him waiting around and seeing what I'm up to, so I'll have to worry about getting home when the time comes.

"Well, I suppose it wouldn't hurt none. I've got a rockin' chair to deliver to Mrs. Brandt up the road. Do we have time to deliver it first?"

"Yeah. That shouldn't be a problem."

Minutes later, with the dresser safely in Aunt Beverly's room, we hop into the Cherokee and head toward Mr. Peterson's house. We load and deliver the rocker and before long we are on our way to the city. The entire ride, I concentrate on anything I can find to keep me in the here and now. Mr. Peterson and I only have so much to talk about, so eventually my attention turns to the road. Counting cars is entertaining for a while—a very short while.

It's not long before my concentration is pulled to the vibration of the vehicle and the blur of white stripes whipping past us on the highway. These are the only details I remember of the trip back from Pittsburgh and, because of that, my mind wants to take me back there. I can feel the tug.

Out of the corner of my eye, the interior of Mr. Peterson's truck shimmers as if I'm looking at it through the heat rising off the grill at a summer barbecue. I close my eyes and concentrate hard on the Jeep Cherokee. I open my eyes just a bit and, afraid to check directly, notice through my peripheral vision that Mr. Peterson's car is back. I take a deep breath.

"You okay?" Mr. Peterson asks.

I turn to look at him, surprised that he noticed anything, and I practically leap from the truck when I see Uncle Clint driving.

"I'm fine," I say, but in my mind I finish the sentence with a rapid, panicked succession of *Mr. Peterson, Mr. Peterson, Mr. Peterson.*

"You don't look so hot," Uncle Clint says.

But was it Uncle Clint? The voice was somewhere in between his and Ray's. The truck keeps alternating between the pickup and the Jeep. I reach out and depress the window button, letting a rush of cool air blow into my face. I take a deep breath, then exhale. I don't have to look. I know I've held on to Mr. Peterson and his Jeep.

"I'm okay," I say.

"Huh?"

"Sorry. I thought you asked me something."

He shakes his head. Trying to break the awkwardness of the moment, I turn on the radio. Tim McGraw. Well, at least it's not Hank Williams, Jr.

The rest of the ride turns out to be the battle of my life. All the stamina, all the willpower that I can muster is barely enough to keep my grip on reality. This is too important to give up on.

"How much farther?" I ask.

Simultaneously, I hear Uncle Clint answer "Too far, quit asking," and Mr. Peterson answer, "About ten minutes."

I focus on Mr. Peterson's voice and use it as a beacon. I continue to ask him questions, some that must seem absolutely random to him. Hell, they seem random to me, but his answers are like Air Traffic Control guiding me in for a landing.

For now, I surge with pride and a feeling that the battle's been won. We are driving along Drennan Road to the front of the terminal and I've never been so happy to see an airport. Still, I'm anxious to get out of the car. The Jeep has barely come to a stop before I'm leaping to the curb and throwing the door closed behind me.

"Whoa, boy. You're gonna get yourself hurt," Mr. Peterson calls.

I stop and take a deep breath. He's right. Though he doesn't know it, I need to seem less conspicuous, not to mention I still have plenty of reservations about being at an airport. That, coupled with my uncle's impending arrival drives my urgent need to disappear quickly and discreetly.

I turn around and lean in through the open car window, giving Mr. Peterson a nod.

"Thanks. This means a lot to me."

"Not a problem, son. You sure you're okay to get home?"

"Yeah. I'm sure."

He nods, gives a friendly smile, then pulls away, leaving me alone at an airport. This is a tremendous step for me. One I will undoubtedly need to share with my psychiatrist.

Swarms of people begin spilling forth from the terminal, indicating that a flight has just arrived and the bags have made it to baggage claim. I imagine the piece of paper that I found in Uncle Clint's jacket and can picture the words "American Airlines" with an arrival time and a flight number (which is neither 11 nor 77, if they even still use those numbers, otherwise I don't think there would have been a force on this earth that could have gotten me to that airport).

Luckily, the terminal is not too big, as airports go, so finding a perch from which to scout Uncle Clint and his mistress should be simple. I weave my way through a sparse crowd toward security, stopping momentarily at the gift shop to purchase a disposable camera. It's early afternoon, so the commuter crowds have come and gone and, being mid-week, the pleasure travelers aren't present. Up ahead, just before the restrooms and the security checkpoint is a small restaurant with a bar. It seems as good a vantage point as any.

I hop onto a stool and ask the bartender for a Pepsi and a cheeseburger. He quickly pours the soda and places it in front of me before heading off to input my order and entertain his more lucrative patrons. This suits me just fine because it leaves me to stare into the crowd without interruption. I glance down at my watch and my stomach begins to tighten. The plane should be landing in just a couple of hours. Soon, Uncle Clint should be here with, I imagine, flowers in hand.

My burger arrives and I take only a bite or two before pushing it aside. I can feel moments of panic poking at my brain before scurrying away, like kids mischievously ringing neighborhood doorbells before fleeing. I do my best to ignore them, just as I would the kids, but some are easier than others. If I expect it, I can prepare to let it pass by, but if I don't, then for all I know it could actually be someone coming to visit and the temptation to open the door is almost too great.

Some time passes, during which I occupy myself with a news report on television. Eventually, I peruse the faces of the crowd, being sure not to glance over my target. Another look at my watch tells me that I've got less than an hour until the flight's arrival. Just as I dig into my pocket to pay for my barely-eaten meal and the three sodas I managed to nurse all this time, in strolls Uncle Clint.

Chapter Twenty-four

I throw some cash on the bar and scurry across the terminal. The sea of people between Uncle Clint and me is made of people of all races, with the exception, as far as I can see, of Middle-Easterners. I don't know that this is always the case in this airport, but it is the case now and I am extremely grateful for it. I have a feeling that once my mission is complete, I'll have a harder time fighting off these flashbacks. I'll lose my focus and continue taking trips back to times in my life when I had absolutely nobody and no reason to go on. I might as well enjoy this as long as I can.

I try to read the look on my uncle's face, but he's not showing much emotion, which isn't all that unusual. He doesn't have flowers which makes me feel a little better. I'm pretty sure he never gave any to Aunt Beverly, so I'd hate to see him be a romantic with some cheap floozy. However, there is *something* in his hand. I shift my position a bit to try to get a better look, but he helps me out by raising the object up to look it over.

A baseball cap.

So he's got himself a sports fan. That's pretty ironic, actually, since the only competition he's ever chosen to observe is the race between his blood pressure and his weight to see which can kill him first.

After a few minutes, he punches his fist into the Colorado Rockies cap to loosen it up, then begins bending the brim. I can't really say for sure, but his actions look like nervous actions. Either he's bored or he's unsettled. The look on his face is not indifference, it's uncertainty. Is he having doubts about his affair?

When the hat concedes, Uncle Clint rolls it up and sticks it into his back pocket. If he was in New York, that hat would be gone already, along with his wallet and possibly even his suspenders.

The crowd in the terminal begins to thicken as the passengers from another flight spill out of the secured area. Uncle Clint rises up on the balls of his feet to look through the mob, but after a second drops back down and pulls the itinerary from his pocket. He must realize that this crowd can't possibly be the flight he's waiting for, because a look of disappointment overtakes his face. It's a look I've seen once before and as soon as I realize when it was that I saw it, I know I have no chance.

Within seconds I'm sitting at a diner somewhere between Pittsburgh and Colorado Springs. It's not that I'm refraining from disclosing the location of the diner, it's that I really don't know where I am. Mile after mile of highway with no distinct characteristic to set it apart from any other highway in America has made it impossible to keep track of our progress. Zoning out for substantial lengths of time hasn't helped either.

Uncle Clint is staring at me across two steaming cups of coffee, a plate of bacon and eggs, and a stack of pancakes. The eggs are his and the pancakes are here only because he insisted. He's practically been putting forkfuls of them into my mouth because I have neither the appetite nor the energy to do it myself.

While his gaze burns into me, I look out the window, hoping to avoid any conversation. In the back of my mind sits an image—an image of an airport which I quickly suppress because it can only cause panic. The world outside is caught in that awkward phase where the streetlights are still on, but the sun has risen enough to paint the world in a steel gray light. There is no movement. It might be Saturday or Sunday. I'm not really sure.

"Here," Uncle Clint murmurs, holding out another forkful of maple syrup-drenched pancakes.

I don't turn my head.

"Boy, you gotta eat," he says, forcefully.

"Why?" I whisper. "What good will it do?"

"Well, it'll keep you alive, for one."

I finally turn toward him and roll my eyes. He puts the fork down on his plate and slouches back in the booth. I can feel him studying me with his eyes.

"What?" I ask in a tone that would have justified him leaning across the table and smacking me in the face.

"How did it get so bad?" he asks, after a moment's hesitation.

I shake my head. It got so bad, so gradually, over such a long period of time that I don't really have an answer for him, so I start from the beginning.

"You should probably listen carefully," I say, "because I'm not coming back."

I'm not sure why I say it or what I mean by it, but he doesn't even react. It's almost like I didn't say it out loud.

Then I begin recounting it all. From where I was on that Tuesday morning in 2001 to the anthrax scares right on to my misadventures with Julius. He doesn't show any emotion during the entire tale, but he also doesn't blink. How about that? I'm riveting.

When I'm finished, I start to sip my coffee, but signal to the waitress for a top-off since it's now ice cold. I wait for my uncle to respond, but in true Uncle Clint fashion, he says nothing.

"What's the matter? Too busy waiting for your mistress?" I ask, immediately slapping my hand over my mouth.

My eyes are wide open in shock while I wait for him to reach across the table and throttle me, but oddly enough, he doesn't react to this either. It's a good thing because I couldn't possibly explain why I said it.

The waitress pours some hot coffee into both our cups and Uncle Clint checks his watch. There still isn't any sign of life outside, so I can't imagine an impending rush hour is any concern.

When the waitress leaves, he asks, "Don't you realize what's happening?"

I'm pretty sure I'm painfully aware of what's happening, but I indulge him with a raised eyebrow.

He leans in close.

"Everything they do, they do to make us afraid. They do these things so we won't live our lives. They're trying to rob us of everything American."

I nod. I know all this, but I let him think he's the first to enlighten me. That's fine.

"We can't let them get the better of us. The more they do, the closer they come to victory."

I snicker, but it's not meant to be rude, it just sneaks out. He glares at me with a look of restrained anger. One that says, *If you weren't mentally handicapped, I'd beat the living crap out of you.*

I quickly and sincerely apologize.

"Listen, Uncle Clint. I get where you're coming from. I really do. Since we walked through the door of the diner, I've determined the ethnic background and likely back-story of fifteen different patrons. I've poked my thigh with a dessert fork at least six times to keep myself from running out of here in absolute terror."

He stares at me, obviously expecting me to spell this out for him.

I take a deep breath before laying it all on the line. "With me, they've won."

No more is said between us—not in the diner and not for the rest of the ride. Well, at least that's how I remember it happening, but this time is different. I'm driving home with Uncle Clint—well it wasn't home yet, but now I call it home—for the second time when I become acutely aware that it *is* the second time. I know it's a flashback, yet I stay right there with my uncle.

I can see every last detail of that long journey but with just a shift in my concentration, I can see Colorado Springs Airport. With Uncle Clint behind the wheel of his brand new truck, I inhale the aroma of my past for what I hope to be the final time.

"Goodbye," I whisper, but not to Uncle Clint. He doesn't hear me anyway.

I focus my attention on the airport and somehow I know that if I can stop being afraid of my future, I can remain in the present and never flash back to the past again. Catching Uncle Clint is important to me because Aunt Bev is all I have left. If he's hurting her, I need to put an end to it. I can't afford to lose her, too.

When I completely banish the past from my perception, Uncle Clint has moved to a bench a few feet away from where he was standing. The baseball cap is back in his hands, but he's pretty much ignoring it. I glance at the arrivals board and notice that the flight we've been waiting for has arrived. Suddenly, my stomach is in knots.

Tearing the camera from its plastic pouch, I creep across the concourse to get a better vantage point from which to take the pictures. The crowd comes in waves, and with each ebb I fix my stare on my uncle. He stands firm against the throng of people anxious to see their loved ones or find their limo driver. Shoulders bump into his shoulders, feet trip over his feet, and a few people manage a last second change of direction in order to avoid running into him face-first.

I glance from him to the oncoming crowd, then back to him, until I notice that he's no longer there. This is it. I walk quickly over to where he was standing and spot the back of his shiny, red head. His hand is in the air, flagging somebody down.

Sweat covers me like the thin layer of water between a diver and his wetsuit. The camera slips from my hand and I almost lose it because I refuse to take my eyes off my uncle. My heart thumps rapidly in my chest as I search blindly along the floor. Finally, my hand comes to rest on the camera. I pick it up and stand. When I do, there is a nest of brown hair draped over Uncle Clint's shoulder. They stand there in their tender embrace, without a care in the world. If only they knew.

I raise the camera, but there are too many people between us. As Clint whispers in her ear, I slip closer. I'm only twenty feet away now.

Fifteen feet.

Ten feet.

I wind the dial on the camera and lift it again. Pressing my eye to the viewfinder, I feel for the button on the top. Just look up. Lift your face and let me get the shot. Nothing, now, can keep me from exposing him. Now Aunt Beverly will know the truth. She'll be hurt, but it's better now than later.

The woman slowly lifts her head from my uncle's shoulder and my finger starts to put pressure on the button. The fact that I'm in an airport has completely escaped me. Terrorism, fear, and paranoia have all left my mind for the time being. For the first time in years, I am completely off-guard.

And that's when I hear it.

"Daddy?"

At first, though the voice comes from just in front of me, I dismiss it. It can't be calling me.

Then the woman on Clint's shoulder reacts to the voice. She snaps her head up and looks to the child, then at me. The camera falls from my hand and now I could care less where it lands or if it gets trampled. For the first time in years, I'm setting my gaze on my beautiful wife. I'm almost afraid to look down, because maybe my son won't be there and when I look back, my wife will be gone, too.

"Becca?" I say, but no sound actually escapes my throat. The only things leaving my body now are tears and strength.

I collapse to my knees and look at the face of my boy. He's grown so much! I can't do anything but put my arms out to him. Before I can brace myself, he crashes into me and wraps his arms around my neck. We both fall to the ground laughing and crying.

"Daddy, I missed you," he keeps saying and I don't know if I'm saying anything at all. Sounds are coming out, but I'm pretty sure they don't resemble any particular language.

Eventually I make my way to my feet, but my grip on Andrew has not loosened a drop. I've got years of hugs to make up for. If I let him go for just a second, I could lose him again.

I wipe the tears from my eyes and take a deep breath. Rebecca is watching us and seems to be just as choked up as we are, but there's also apprehension that's as visible as her clothes, hair, and make-up.

"Hi, Jim," she mouths.

I look at Uncle Clint who hasn't cracked a tear, a smile, or even taken a swing at me. He looks me in the eye and I can read his thoughts. *Don't screw this up.*

Damn good advice.

"Thank you," I say to my uncle, but he waves it off and walks off, leaving me alone with Andrew and Rebecca.

My wife and I still stand ten feet apart, but our eyes are in constant contact. Releasing one arm from around my son, I extend it to her. She hits me a little more gently than Andrew did, but it feels just as good. I have a feeling we'll be right in this spot through a few more arrivals. Besides, after we finally stop hugging, we've got about forty-five minutes of Hank Williams, Jr. to look forward to and I'm in no hurry.

Chapter Twenty-five

I was right about one thing: Aunt Beverly was completely surprised by the arrival of our guests. Apparently, Uncle Clint had not said a word to her in order to avoid raising her hopes in case something didn't work out. I introduce her to her great-nephew and they hit it off right away. This is good because it gives Rebecca and me a chance to excuse ourselves to talk.

We sneak into my room and shut the door behind us. I can't help but plant a full, passionate kiss on her lips. She responds for a moment, but then pushes me away with a laugh.

"Settle down. Let's ease back into this."

"I just missed you guys so much."

"And we missed you, but we've got a lot to talk about."

"Why did you come back?" I ask.

She grabs my hand and sits me down on the edge of the bed. "I got into a relationship and the whole time all I could think about was you. Drew never took to the guy anyway."

I smile at this, my heart warming, even though I'm sure there is much more to the story.

"Listen, all this will come in due time. Let's just enjoy the fact that we're back together right now, okay? There's going to be a lot of work.

I need to be able to better handle your condition and you're going to need to work on trusting me again. For now, let's put our past in the past."

I nod, but I know I can't do that. Not yet. She can obviously see the concern on my face because she asks what's wrong. I reach into my back pocket and pull out the detective's business card.

"There's something I have to do." No matter what this Matthew wants, I have to talk to him. I can't imagine it's a trick to arrest me or issue a summons; the detective could have served me with papers when he was first here if that was his objective. Even if that was what was going to happen, at this point I have to do it.

"We'll do it together," she offers. "Whatever it is."

"No. Not this one. I need to do this to put my past in the past." I hesitate, then add, "I have to be honest. There could be some bad outcomes here. Really bad."

She raises one eyebrow to inquire about what's going on, but at the same time her shoulders slump, defeated. She must feel like she's done all this only to find out it could all be for nothing.

I place my hand to the side of her face and look her in the eye. Then, I proceed to tell her the whole story. When I'm finished, she is dead silent.

"I need you to understand that this is something I have to do."

Slowly, she nods. "Okay, but I'm not going anywhere. I know that might be hard to believe right now, but I'm not. I'm here if you need me."

I give her another kiss and this time she melts into my arms. It feels incredible and at this moment I can't imagine how I was ever able to fail to perform for her. We kiss for another minute then separate.

After she goes out to join the family—*our family*—I pick up the phone and make the call. Apparently, Matthew has made a trip out here and is eager to meet with me, so I make the arrangements. Within an hour, the two of us are sitting at the dining room table. I recognize Matthew now and we greet each other with a bit of apprehension.

"Jim," he says, "I'm going to get right to it. Julius is about to be set free."

My body shudders at the words.

"I can see you feel the same way about that as the rest of us do. If he is set free, there's no telling what he'll do to any of us, or our families. I have reason to believe he knew a hell of a lot more about us than we knew about him, or each other for that matter."

"He was much smarter than he let on, that's true. But how is this possible? I thought he had fifteen years for racially biased aggravated manslaughter and another fifteen for conspiracy to commit murder."

"Ruling was recently overturned on appeal. His lawyer managed to convince the judge that Julius' confession was obtained under duress or some such shit. He's convinced a court that there were others involved that masterminded the whole thing—that he was just an innocent bystander to the whole event. He even got them to believe that he didn't know why he was supposed to find the second guy. Told the court that we told him he was supposed to contact us once he found him. He says he was set up."

"But the second guy. Couldn't he testify …"

"Unconscious at the time, remember? Besides, he doesn't have any real insight into who was behind this. He just knows he was attacked by an angry mob."

I begin to feel nauseous.

"What can we do?" I ask.

"Testify. Come back to New York and testify."

The words are like a freight train careening through my skull. Go back to New York? I can't. There's no way. I'm just getting better. My family is back. I have an incredible sense of vertigo as images of the sky high buildings seem to tower over me right here in Aunt Beverly's dining room. I still see lower Manhattan as a dust filled island with debris raining down. I'm shaking my head from side to side.

"But he's been tried already," I stammer. "Double jeopardy, right? Can't be tried again for the same crime?"

"If new evidence arises, he can. Testimony of the people that were there that day is certainly new evidence."

I get up from the chair and walk around, their eyes never leaving me.

"I don't know if I can do this," I say.

"Jim, we've all got something to lose if this doesn't happen, but we are in agreement that if just one of us won't do it, we all won't do it. Just remember, though, he's a madman, Jim."

"It's not that. It's just that, well, New York ..." but I trail off. I'm standing in the doorway looking at my wife and son playing Yahtzee with Aunt Beverly and I know I have to do this. For them. For me. It needs to be done. Despite my fears, it has to happen. If it doesn't, then I'll never be able to sleep at night knowing that I've put my family in danger. It's not easy, but I force myself to get a grip on my emotions. I sweep the images to the recesses of consciousness and do everything I can to lock them there.

I turn back to Matthew and reply, voice cracking, "Okay. I guess I'll do it. We've got to make this right."

EPILOGUE

———————— ▼ ————————

The trip to New York was difficult, but I did it with my family at my side. I fought panic attacks and an occasional flashback, but never once let one overcome me. Rebecca was a rock for me. Something about her had changed over the few years that we were apart. She apparently had a tremendous amount of guilt over not sticking by me, but I try to ease that burden by telling her I understand why she left.

The trial went well. Not only are we optimistic about keeping Julius behind bars, but Matthew's lawyer was able to strike a deal to get us immunity in exchange for testifying. As I sit on the wooden bench in the courtroom, awaiting the verdict, I notice the hush that has fallen over the spectators. There are a few whispered conversations, mostly by people in the back of the room who probably have no direct relation to the case, but we sit in silence, our hands intertwined with those of our loved ones, drawing on their strength and courage. A few moments later, deliberations over, the jury returns to the courtroom. I'm literally sitting on the edge of my seat as if getting closer to the jury will help me hear the verdict sooner.

"Mr. Foreman, have you reached a verdict?" the judge asks.

"We have, Your Honor."

The foreman is a tall, wiry black man with bits of gray sprouting over his temples. The rest of the jury is made up of a pretty diverse racial mix, which all along has made us feel like we had an advantage. As I hold my breath through the foreman's pause, I pray we were right. During the pause, the foreman hands a piece of paper to the bailiff who presents it to the judge. Right there, on that small slip of paper, is the future of my family.

The judge reads the note and nods to the foreman, then he looks up from the bench, specifically at Julius. The prosecutor, defense attorney, and defendant take this as their cue to stand.

The judge clears his throat, then says, "On count one, the charge of aggravated manslaughter, how does the jury find?"

"The jury finds the defendant guilty as charged, Your Honor."

There is a roar from the crowd, mostly in approval. After a quick glance around the room, I decide it is completely in approval. Throughout the trial, nobody has offered any support for Julius. He apparently has nobody that cares enough to be here for him. It isn't long ago that I would have felt sorry for him, but not now. The judge smacks the gavel down three times and orders us to quiet down.

"On the second count, the charge of conspiracy to commit murder," he continues, "how does the jury find?"

"The jury finds the defendant guilty as charged, Your Honor."

Now the roar is a blend of approval and relief. Julius just stares straight ahead, an angry, defiant look on his face. We are up on our feet now, congratulating each other, shaking hands, hugging. Men I knew by first name only or by online ID's until just a few months ago now seem like buddies with which I've been to war. We know we're not about to pick up and begin having monthly get-togethers, but there is a bond now that can't be broken—a bond forged by mistakes made in a hellish time, but strengthened by good choices made in an attempt to set things right.

As we celebrate, an Arab woman dressed in black approaches. It may be traditional dress, but it has the feeling of something worn by some-one in mourning. Suddenly, the high fives and pats on the back seem empty. For a moment we almost forgot that there was a man who didn't come through this. Then I see the Arab couple behind the woman. The man is the survivor of our attack. Silence and shame overcome us.

The woman can only be in her late twenties, but her eyes seem to be laden with the experiences of a much older person. She tries to speak, but struggles. Eventually, she manages to say, "Thank you."

Her eyes well up with tears, but she manages to hold them back. "Today this man who took my husband from me could have been free. I know you were all there when it happened, you were all a part of it, but I also know that you could have remained anonymous and let this man be free. For that, I thank you."

We all nod and murmur responses to the woman, nobody comfortable with the idea of uttering a "You're welcome." We stand for a moment in awkward silence. Looking around the courtroom, I make eye contact with Julius who is being led away by the bailiffs. He resists enough to make them stop. I want to avert my eyes, disappear into the crowd, do anything but stand here beneath his glare, but I hold my ground.

He seems surprised by this. "You're a traitor, you son-of-a-bitch. When I get out ..."

"Shut up, Julius," I interrupt. Nobody is more surprised than I am. These are the first words I've uttered to this man in years—this man who haunts my dreams (and flashbacks) to this day. My words are wrought with anger, but I manage to stay calm. I don't know where the courage is coming from, but I roll with it. "Shut up and go to Hell."

I'm not sure if it is my imagination, but he seems a bit smaller after that, a bit broken. Satisfied and filled with a small degree of pride, I take my wife's hand and lead her out of the courtroom.

*   *   *   *

The sentence turns out to be thirty years, as it was before the appeal, and the group has made a pact to return for every parole hearing to do our best to keep Julius where he belongs. Maybe over time the trips will get easier. Maybe not.

Now, back in Colorado Springs, Rebecca and I sit side by side on the back step of the farmhouse, watching Andrew run around the yard with our new Black Lab, Jet. The name is not unintentional. To the uninterested it's a reference to his color, but to us it's a subtle reminder of what drove us apart so that we can keep it from ever happening again.

The winter has come and gone and the summer is growing old, too. Aunt Beverly and Uncle Clint have been kind enough to allow us to continue to use their spare rooms until we're on our feet. Hopefully, that won't be too long. I've been working a job steadily since December.

Jet races directly toward Andrew after retrieving a stick, but veers off at the last moment, forcing Andrew to go chasing after him. I could watch this all night. They'd pass out exhausted long before I would.

I still see Dr. Wallace every week and even he's noted my marked improvement. On top of that, Rebecca and I go to couple's therapy. We keep our eyes on Andrew, but he hasn't really given us any reason to think he needs to see somebody. He just seems so happy to have his parents back together, the rest of the world be damned.

"Dinner!" Aunt Beverly calls as she sets a bowl of fresh fruit salad onto the picnic table. The spring breeze flutters her house dress about.

Andrew rushes to the table where he promptly receives a scolding for not first going to wash the filthy dog slobber off his hands. Rebecca and I take our seats and Uncle Clint joins us a few moments later. We each stave off our ferocious appetites as Aunt Beverly parades one bountiful plate after another onto the red wooden tabletop.

The aroma of fried chicken and biscuits is mouth-watering and the sneaking suspicion that there might be some homemade funnel cakes waiting for the good little boys and girls who finish their entire meals makes it almost impossible not to inhale a plateful at a time. Despite all this, we each keep our hands folded neatly in our laps until Aunt Beverly places the lemonade pitcher on the table and takes her seat (we'd offer to help, but found it, long ago, to be fruitless).

Andrew returns and we all take each others hands and bow our heads. Normally, Uncle Clint would say Grace, muttering his "Bless us O Lord, for these thy gifts and so on and so forth," but I clear my throat before he gets the chance to begin. This is something I've been meaning to do for a long time now, but I just haven't been able to find the words. Tonight is different. Tonight, as the sun begins its descent to the Rockies and the hot summer air begins to cool, the words seem obvious. I don't have to ask permission. The fact that Uncle Clint hasn't yet started means he's expecting me to pray.

"Heavenly Father," I begin, "thank you for this beautiful meal you've placed before us on this perfect summer evening. Thank you for the family that sits around this table and the immeasurable love that grows here. Please let us all remain together."

I feel Rebecca's hand close tightly around mine. The sensation is all I can focus on for the next few moments, but somehow I finish the blessing with an "Amen."

Well, at least I say amen and my son, wife and aunt all say amen. Uncle Clint, however, apparently not realizing that my prayer was coming to an end, bursts out with, "We get the picture, can we eat now?"

He turns a bit red when he realizes what's happened, but the sudden permission to eat quickly makes him forget any embarrassment. He adds his amen and begins digging in. Dinner conversation is light and plentiful. There are no awkward silences.

The meal ends and Rebecca helps Aunt Beverly clean up. She'll let my wife bring plates to the kitchen, but that's where it ends. Rebecca doesn't dare scrape food from the plates.

When the sun begins to set, Rebecca gets Andrew ready for bed and I light a fire outside. As I stare up to the clear night sky and listen to the crackle of the flames, I feel a pair of arms wrap around my waist. A moment later, a pair of lips nuzzles into the crook of my neck.

"Hurry it up, will you," I whisper. "My wife will be back any second."

She gives me a smack on the butt and lets out a little laugh.

"I missed you, Jim," she says, as I turn to look into her sparkling eyes.

"I missed you, too. Both of you. These past few months feel like a dream."

She nods but assures me that it is very real.

"You know," she says, "if it wasn't for your uncle, I might never have come back."

"Yeah, he did a great thing."

"Before I left," she says, leading me by the hand to two chairs by the fire, "I gave him a number at which he could reach me in the event of an emergency."

"Like if I slit my wrists or threw myself in front of a bus?"

"Among other things," she replies, without skipping a beat. She's become re-accustomed to my deranged sense of humor. That's a good thing.

"He called me a couple of weeks after you got back here. He said you were having a lot of trouble and could use my company and support."

I nod, my opinion of Uncle Clint growing stronger by the moment. "He has very strong beliefs about family."

"I couldn't do it, though. Not then, but I did begin keeping in touch. The longer I went without talking to him, the more I would think and worry about you. I think your uncle was fully aware of this and kept his eye out for just the right time to take advantage of it. He's smarter than you give him credit for."

She grabs my hand, but we both continue to stare ahead into the fire. We both know that this story ends in a good way, but the journey to that end is still a bit painful for both of us.

We fall silent for the better part of an hour, only occasionally stirring to poke at the fire. My arm is wrapped around her shoulder. A heavy sigh tells me that she's got more to say.

"Jim, I just feel so terrible for everything I ..."

I press a finger to her lips to keep her from completing the thought. She looks up into my eyes, but I refuse to give her any reason to continue.

"Becca, you need to stop," I tell her. "I'm going to say this just this one time, so please listen. I don't care what happened back then. I don't care that you left and I don't care what kind of condition I was in. The fact is that it's in the past. There's nothing we can do to change it. I don't care how you came back or why. I've thanked Uncle Clint in my own way and I'm sure I will continue to thank him for years and years to come. All I know is that I can now go to sleep at night knowing that when I wake up, I will be able to spend time with my wife and son."

Tears are welling up in her eyes, but she doesn't say a word.

"Besides," I continue with a wry smile, "if you keep obsessing about leaving me, you're going to make me paranoid."

978-0-595-47852-1
0-595-47852-2